RACHEL'S STORY

KINGFISHER
An imprint of Kingfisher Publications Plc
New Penderel House, 283–288 High Holborn
London WC1V 7HZ
www.kingfisherpub.com

First published by Kingfisher 2006
2 4 6 8 10 9 7 5 3 1

A CIP catalogue record for this book
is available from the British Library.

ISBN-13: 978-0-7534-1326-5
ISBN-10: 0 7534 1326 4

Printed in India
1TR/0206/THOM/SGCH/80GSMSTORA/C

MY SIDE OF THE STORY

The Plague

RACHEL'S STORY

PHILIP WOODERSON

KINGFISHER

Read Rachel's story first, then flip over
and read Robert's side of the story!

Chapter One

Until one day in late May, I'd never thought of the plague as something that might hurt me.

It was more like the stench in the air we breathed, something we had to put up with when it was hot in the city.

My mother kept quiet about it, the one thing she did keep quiet about, as if to convince herself it would never affect folk like us, only the poorest people squashed into their festering hovels, along with their chickens and pigs. She had much bigger concerns than the plague – like making our house *à la mode*.

My father had his hands full with keeping his business going, even with help from Robert, his far-from-humble assistant. Robert lived in our house and looked down his nose at us all. Not that he had any right to. He was my country cousin, come to London 'to make his fortune'. He was less than two years older than me, but thought he knew so much more – not just about Father's business but everything else in the universe, including the war with the Dutch.

He said there'd be nothing to stop them sailing up the river and blowing up London Bridge.

"We wouldn't have got in this mess," Father said, "not under Oliver Cromwell."

I'd been too young to remember such times. I was born on the day King Charles I was executed at Whitehall by Oliver Cromwell's men. It had been such an icy day, the King had needed to wear two shirts to stop himself from shivering, not wanting the crowds to think he might have been scared of the axe. Or so my father insisted.

But I digress. What I meant to say was how my mother believed that my being born on that day had made me 'the trouble I am'. Stubborn, she said, and head-strong. Words just as suited to Robert!

We disagreed all the time.

I disagreed that morning about Father's latest venture. He was selling a load of cloth to his rival, Giles Pethbridge. Robert thought this a wise idea, sure to bring in extra profits without much extra labour. But I didn't trust Giles Pethbridge.

As soon as they'd gone to the warehouse to supervise the delivery, Mother appeared in the parlour. She was dressed as if to go out for one of her card-playing parties, though she said she was staying at home. "I have an appointment," she said.

"Who with?"

"Oh, only Signor Giorgio. You know, dear, the master plasterer. I want him to give me an estimate for doing our dining room ceiling."

The old one looked perfectly fine to me, but she wanted a 'stucco frieze depicting grapes and vine leaves'.

And then she really surprised me. "You can go to the market without me," she said. "I'm sure you'll be safe with Jess."

Jess was our household servant, but also my best bosom friend. She was almost two years older than me, but we had the same sense of humour. So it was blissful to be with her, without my mother to get in the way, telling me where not to look and how to be ladylike.

Jess spotted Doctor Bead.

He was our local Apothecary. He claimed to have found the cure for every sickness and palsy to be found in the City of London – in the shape of his own Universal Pill – to be had for a sizeable price.

The doctor was waddling in front of us now, wearing some tight new breeches, his paunch sticking out at the front and his long hands clasped behind his back, like one of those pelican birds I'd seen in the menagerie at St Bartholemew Fayre.

I was making a great imitation, expecting Jess to laugh, when she grabbed at my elbow – "Look, Rachel."

We were near the end of our street, on the corner by The Sun Tavern. We lived in Gracechurch Street.

Our house was across the street from my father's warehouse and shop. The street was narrow and crowded, jammed with baggage and carts. You had to watch where you put your feet, as the channel ran down the middle was an open gutter. Nearly all the houses belonged to rich merchants like us, and the one Jess was pointing at belonged to some fair-headed Swedes who traded in jute from the Baltic.

A yellow cross was daubed on the door.

Their haughty daughter Ingrid always carried a prayer book on Sunday, and she was pious enough, but I couldn't imagine she'd want to paint a cross on their front door!

A scrap of paper was pinned underneath, with these words written in black: *God have mercy on us*.

"What does that mean?" I asked Jess.

Jess explained what it meant. Her brother Toby had told her about a new law that was passed by the mayor. "You have to paint a cross on your door if your house is infected with plague. As a warning for folks to keep clear."

"So one of their servants has got it," I said. "How awful. I'd better tell Father."

Back home, when I told him at dinner, Father explained very gently, "It wasn't a servant, Rachel.

8

Miss Ingrid, she died in the night. The first death from plague in the neighborhood, and God be willing, the last!"

I was too stunned to answer. I'd never liked Ingrid that much. Even so, she'd been younger than me by three weeks, with blue eyes and a fine complexion.

Mother hastily changed the subject. I hardly heard what she said. It was just about 'Signor Giorgio'. He'd given her his estimate for the new dining room ceiling.

She'd already spent Father's money on having the woodwork painted. A strapping great German called Gerhard had kept Mother cheerful last summer, covering up the oak panels with pictures of cows and milkmaids.

Father squinted at Giorgio's estimate. "My eyeglasses – where have they got to?"

We all made helpful suggestions because it wasn't the first time he'd forgotten where he had left them. But Robert had the answer. "You must have left them this morning on Mr Pethbridge's desk, when you got up to greet Lord Beastor."

"Lord Beastor was there?" Mother prompted, impressed by the very name. "His uncle's the Earl of Styx, I believe. A very grand figure at Court. Our Mr Pethbridge must be on the rise!"

Giles Pethbridge had started off as my father's first humble clerk. He had left to start on his own when an aunt had died, leaving him money. The man had a stodgy face, with greedy eyes and sneering lips and a pointy beard in the Dutch style to cover his round, flabby chin.

But as Robert pointed out, Pethbridge moved with the times. In five years he'd built a great business, dealing in fancy French fabrics – and now, to add to his profits, he was buying plain cloths from my father, 'merely as ballast, dear sir, so the French ship won't return empty.' A sore point with my mother, as Father's trade had been in decline ever since his own father died. But again, as Robert would have it, no one could make a fortune dealing in plain English cloths while the customers were old misers who made their plain clothes last a lifetime. Mr Pethbridge attracted the rich, who changed their clothes every season.

"Why don't you be kind," I said, "and go back and fetch Father's glasses?"

Robert flashed me a withering glance. "Yes, of course. I'd be pleased to, Mr Hopgood."

He had to deliver a letter to one of Father's customers on the south side of the river. He promised to look in on Pethbridge before he came back to our shop. But he didn't get back for his afternoon stint, or for his supper that evening.

Next morning he still wasn't back.

My father was baffled by it. "Always such a reliable fellow…"

Mother said she'd had a suspicion he wouldn't be with us for long. "He's got such clever ideas in his head."

"Thoughtful, I grant you," said Father, "but shouldn't we look for him somewhere?"

"He probably just met a friend."

"He hasn't got friends," I put in.

Father went round to Pethbridge's warehouse, only to come back and tell me Robert had never turned up there.

"But what about your glasses? You picked them up?" Mother enquired.

"We looked, but we couldn't find them, my dear."

"And Mr Pethbridge, what did he say?"

"He suggested Robert went drinking."

"But he never drinks," I said.

"Or else to the theatre. There is a theatre in Southwark not far from my customer's house."

"I don't see how that explains him not coming back last night. Any case, Father, you know very well, Robert couldn't afford the theatre. He's saving up every penny. He's hardly a gad about town!"

11

In fact, he seemed to spend his free time with his nose always buried in books, either Father's account books or else the single book he had brought with him from home – a thick volume by Francis Bacon.

"Perhaps he's gone back to Saxton." Father said this without much conviction, knowing as well as I did, Robert had never been happy living under his stepfather's roof. He'd seen London as his big chance to make his own way in the world. That was why he had put up with living with us and drudging away in our warehouse.

"Perhaps he got offered a much better job by someone important," I said.

"I'm sure he'd have told us," said Father.

So then Father made some enquiries of street traders, neighbours and colleagues. His customer in Southwark confirmed he'd received the letter. But no one had anything new to add as to why Robert might have gone missing.

Mother said we'd be foolish to worry. "The only reason we hired him was because of my sister, Martha. She made a mess of her own life, getting involved with his father, that penniless fool of an artist. No wonder the boy's let us down!"

"That remains to be seen, my dear Betsy."

"Well, he hasn't come back, there's no doubt

of that!"

"I just hope he isn't in trouble."

The days passed, but still we heard nothing. At the end of the week, Father told us he was writing a letter to Saxton asking if Robert was home. Two weeks later, we heard from his mother that she'd had nothing from Robert since he had set off for London. But by this time we had other worries. The city was buzzing with rumours of a great battle at sea between our ships and the Dutch. There were fears we had been defeated.

"If this should be so," said Father, "it would be a terrible judgment on our degenerate Court and all those fashionable fops in their fine French velvets and lace." Then Pethbridge brought us the news, fresh from his 'patron', Lord Beastor, that the Duke of York had done gloriously well and beaten the Dutch fleet off Lowestoft. Their flagship had been exploded; our nation was safe again.

"Except from the pestilence," Father griped back.

"Oh, that needn't worry us," Pethbridge replied. "In fact, Mr Hopgood, I come here tonight not just to speak of our victory but on a new matter of business. If we two can have a short private talk, I think it might profit you greatly!"

Chapter Two

The next day we had a visit from the local constable. "Your spectacles, sir. They were handed to me by a fellow named Simon Slop. A lowly sort, but you know him, I think?"

Simon had been a slop man, collecting waste from our cesspit. But such a friendly fellow Father had taken him on to lift bolts of cloth round our warehouse. Then Simon had left to help Pethbridge.

'Slop the traitor', as mother described him.

"He came and told me," the constable said, "he found them up the street, sir, in the gutter outside The Sun Tavern."

"But how did he guess they were mine?" Father asked.

"Says he saw your assistant drop them."

Now naturally this made Mother chirp up that Robert must have gone drinking and got taken up with 'bad company'. But what she couldn't explain was how Robert had got Father's glasses to lose if he'd not been to Pethbridge's warehouse.

"Why didn't he bring them back straight away?" Father wanted to know.

"Claimed he'd been sick," said the Constable.

"But doesn't he want a reward?"

"Didn't say."

"Well, good old Slop," said Father.

A few days after this, there was a general thanksgiving for our victory over the Dutch, with bonfires and street celebrations. There were parties all over the city. We went to one on Finsbury Field. Father paid for much of the food and drink, and Pethbridge claimed the credit. But I got my own back by asking him how Slop had managed to find Father's glasses if Robert hadn't collected them.

I saw how his face reacted in the light of the flames from the bonfire.

Mother told me to mind my manners.

"No, ma'am, I will answer your daughter." He did so, with the stupid idea that Father had dropped the glasses himself on his way home from the warehouse.

"Not by The Sun Tavern," I said. "That's in the wrong direction."

"Well, maybe the boy had them all the time and threw them away," declared Pethbridge. "You don't think I put them out there?"

"We just want to know about Robert – what happened to him."

"He'll be fine. Crafty fellow like that, a born climber."

"Untrustworthy," Mother agreed. "Now why don't you tell us some more, sir, about your business proposal?"

"Indeed." Pethbridge looked delighted. He'd clearly formed the impression Father was not to be shifted. "There's a growing demand for fine fabrics in this great city of ours, as I'm sure you can see, Mrs Hopgood. Your husband could share in this trade. A very good way to begin, I believe, at a very small cost to himself, would be if he takes a small portion of my next consignment. It should be arriving from France quite soon. I'd be delighted to help him this way, as he helped me when I first started."

"How sensible, don't you agree, John?"

"Not sensible while we're at war with the Dutch, and the French might join them against us."

"But if Mr Pethbridge feels it is safe, why shouldn't *you*?" said Mother.

My father kept shaking his head. He was bald on top but did not wear a wig, and the fluffy strands round the back of his head had turned almost white this last year, though his eyebrows had stayed bushy black. As always, he wore a plain shirt of white cloth, a black coat and simple black breeches, in contrast to Mr Pethbridge, whose collar and cuffs dripped with fashionable lace, and whose coat was of bright turquoise satin.

"The Dutch were defeated," said Pethbridge. "That's why we're here celebrating."

"One battle does not win the war, Giles, and then there's the plague," mumbled Father. "Your clients are fleeing the city."

"Because of the heat," declared Pethbridge. "But when they come back, they'll be twice as keen to catch up on what they've been missing. My business is with the gentry, but if you'd like to take some of my cheaper fabrics, they're sure to find plenty of takers with well-to-do merchants' wives. Such as yourself, Mrs Hopgood, a lady of taste and discernment. And I won't charge a penny up front because Mr Hopgood has credit, what with the cloths he's supplied me."

"For which you've not paid me," said Father.

"So then we'd be quits," declared Pethbridge. "But you, sir, would double your profit, as I told you the other evening."

Mother was nodding her head at this, so I was relieved to hear Father say he could not get involved.

"Not in something I don't understand. As I answered you then, Mr Pethbridge, I don't know a fig about fashions."

"You should trust your good wife!" declared Pethbridge.

Mother simpered, but Father bristled. Pethbridge sensed he had gone too far. He took a step back from the fire, watching some revellers dancing, then noticed Doctor Bead nearby, warming his tapering fingers.

"Lord Beastor's physician," said Pethbridge to me. "The fellow's a medical genius. Cut a gallstone the size of a duck's egg out of Lady Dalmeeny. I must go and congratulate him."

As soon as he'd gone, Father took a deep breath, and Mother tugged at my arm. "One day, when you're older, Rachel, you might make a match with a man like that; a most advantageous one too."

Back home I stalked off upstairs, intending to sit in my room. This room was part of the attic. I had to share it with Jess, though I was lucky enough to have the comfortable bed, while she had to sleep on the truckle, except in the cold of winter when we shared my bed to keep warm. On the left was a smaller room shared by Cook and her husband, Joe, who'd moved in when Slop departed. On the right was a thin partition wall through which we could hear the two servants next door giggling about their mistress, the elderly Widow Blunket.

Robert had slept downstairs, behind a curtain in the lobby next to the kitchen door.

As I lay on my bed and thought about him, I wondered if Pethbridge was right. Had Robert got bored and moved on? I thought of his few possessions, none of them worth very much, though surely of value to him. He'd surely have wanted to take them.

I went down and pulled back the curtain.

His travelling chest was there; his clothing was still inside it. But so was the small, framed portrait depicting his mother, my aunt.

His father, an unsuccessful artist who had died when Robert was three, had painted the likeness. Robert had treasured that picture. It was all he had left of his father, except for a set of volumes written by Francis Bacon – a great philosopher, so Robert claimed. There was one in the chest, *The New Atlantis*. He'd quoted from it at mealtimes, much to my mother's annoyance.

Why hadn't he wanted to take all these things? Perhaps he'd been bought some new clothes if he'd found a generous employer. He'd survive without Francis Bacon. But he would have taken that portrait.

That proved he had not meant to leave.

I hurried back to the front parlour. "Father," I said, "you must find Simon Slop and ask him more about how it was he came to pick up your glasses."

"But my dear, it was perfectly simple."

"I'm worried. I'm sure of one thing. Robert never intended to leave. That means he couldn't come back because something terrible happened. Like an accident. Or he was robbed and he tried to fight back and... "

"The constable would have heard, dear."

"Or else he got sick," I added.

"Went wandering where he shouldn't have done, caught the plague," my mother put in. She went 'humph'. It was almost a laugh. She had drunk too much sack at the party.

I moved across to the front window.

Outside it was almost dark, but thanks to all the candles our neighbours had put in their windows to celebrate winning the battle, I saw the last of the revellers dancing in a line down the street. And in a dark doorway, I saw someone else – an angular figure in black. For an instant I thought it was Robert, his face hidden under a hood. But as he stepped forwards, I realized the man was too tall and thin. And somehow sinister too. Instinctively I looked away, not wanting to meet his gaze. And when I glanced back he was gone.

I heard a harsh rap on the door. I rushed to open it, heart beating hard, but it was only Jess back from the bonfire party, pink cheeked and smiling broadly. Until she saw me – then her face fell. "Why, Rachel, you look as pale as death!"

Chapter Three

Pale as death? I was full of life, though Mother had made me wonder if Robert might truly be dead.

Taken ill of the plague, unable to walk, curling up in a squalid doorway?

That night I lay in bed dreaming up the most terrible fates, my thoughts slipping out of focus until I was caught up in a fantasy of Pethbridge standing on London Bridge, pointing down at the dirty green water as Robert's bloated body floated by on the ebbing tide.

I jerked awake.

Why bring in Pethbridge?

Jess stirred, reaching out a hand.

Dear Jess. She tried to cheer me up, falling back on her usual trick of relaying what Toby, her brother, had said about his employer – Pethbridge, man of the future – some of it scurrilous stuff. But tonight I did not find it funny.

"So what's the matter?" Jess asked.

I sat up in bed in the darkness. "The plague... if you catch it, does it take long, I mean to – you know – if it kills you?"

She spluttered. "You gloomy thing. You don't have

to worry your head with that. It's not for young ladies like you!"

"But Ingrid died. Now her parents are dead. Dr Bead told my father this evening."

"Her father had a big warehouse down on Lower Thames Street, a filthy festering place," said Jess. "Not surprising he picked up bad germs."

"My father goes down to the river as well."

And then I thought of Robert delivering that letter on the far side of London Bridge, and understood what my dream meant. In a flash I had the image of Robert taken ill, stumbling and falling over.

As if reading my mind, Jess turned over, propping her head with one hand and facing me in the dark. "It can strike mighty fast, that's for certain. Toby and Mr Pethbridge were crossing the river last week, taking the ferry from Queenshithe. Toby said the boatman was hearty when they started out, but he was too feeble to pull the oars by the time he was halfway across. Toby had to take over."

I kept quiet, waiting for more.

"So when they got back, Mr Pethbridge went straight to Dr Bead and came back with two Universals. Swallowed them both, then was sick as a dog, and serves him right too, says I!"

She giggled. "And Rachel, I told you about that

boy chimney sweep?"

I shook my head.

"I didn't? Well, listen to this then. Poor brat. Struck ill while stuck up a chimney at the fish-smoking shed by Moon Steps. You'd think the smoke would have cured him!" She laughed again, but this time she broke off with a sigh and a nudge. "I'm sorry, Rachel. Not funny."

Next morning, down in the parlour, I heard Father telling Mother the weekly bills of mortality for the last week of June showed 300 dead of the plague inside the old City walls. "And the Court is said to be on the move from Whitehall to Hampton Court. It's enough to make me feel it's not wise to extend ourselves with Pethbridge's fancy fabrics. He keeps on at me, wants a decision."

Mother scalded him. "You're so feeble, never willing to rise to a challenge. The plague will be over and life will go on, with you grumbling about our expenses while Mr Pethbridge gets even richer!"

Father bowed his head but said nothing.

I cornered him on his own later on and gave him a questioning look.

And then with a twitchy expression, making his

eyebrows come together, he said that I shouldn't worry, at least about our business, as stocks of black cloth and white linen were shifting remarkably fast right now, thanks to demand for mourning clothes and winding sheets for the corpses.

But I didn't care about business. After the thanksgiving party, I'd asked him about Simon Slop, the man who had found his glasses. "Have you managed to talk to him yet?"

Father looked even less comfy. "It seems, from what Pethbridge tells me, Slop wasn't quite up to the mark. Not punctual, too fond of his ale. He had to be fired from his job."

"But when?"

"Soon after the thanksgiving party."

"But can't he be traced?"

"It seems not."

I went and told Jess about this, to ask her what Toby might add. She teased me about my 'obsession'. "You're like a love-sick maid. I bet your 'sweetheart' Robert ran after some fine piece of stuff more buxom than you, and you're jealous!"

"Stupid, Jess, don't talk like a fish wife! You know Robert wasn't like that."

"Ooh, don't be coy, he was handsome enough!"

"Don't say *you* were soft for him, Jess?"

"That's better, still able to jest then!"

I sighed. I was starting to doubt it. I felt so cooped up, so frustrated.

So little went on in our house.

My mother kept preening on about Pethbridge's generous offer, while Father prevaricated, and time kept drifting by, and we heard more and more of the plague.

Towards the end of July, I overheard my father exclaiming under his breath that the weekly bills of mortality showed an alarming increase. "1,090 for last week. Now it's 1,700. And the King's quitting Hampton Court today. He's taking the Court to Salisbury."

"Then we should leave too," said my mother, "when you've settled with Mr Pethbridge. Then you'll have some new stock for the autumn, for when we come back. Get a move on!"

Father said he was wondering about this. The best thing might be for Mother and I to go to stay with her sister, while he stayed to safeguard the warehouse.

"I'm not going *there*!" exclaimed Mother.

"I wouldn't mind going," I told him.

"You would when you got there," said Mother. "The middle of nowhere, back of beyond! Silly girl. I worry about you."

"No, you worry about plastering ceilings," I said. "I'm worried about catching plague!"

And then on the following morning, we received an invitation to visit Pethbridge's warehouse to admire his latest consignment, including the cargo for Father, only just landed from France.

It was a hot afternoon. I wanted to stay at home, but Mother was of the opinion here was a useful chance for me to practise some courtesy. I feared it was more than that. As Jess put it, only half joking, "You might make a good wife one day. Just think, what a useful alliance – Pethbridge and Hopgood, drapers!"

Not funny. It made me feel sick.

Though on the other hand, I felt I was going with Mother to act as her chaperone. She took so much trouble arranging her dress, pinning the skirts at the front to show off her underskirts, then painting her face with white lead. And when we finally got there, she was simpering like a young maiden in front of that horrible man.

But perhaps I should blame the vapours, for as we walked along Gracechurch Street, Mother took the precaution of holding a shawl to her face. It was soaked in a compound of brandy, spices, horse urine and herbs, recommended by Dr Bead as an unfailing

27

protection against infected air. She'd tried to persuade me to try it myself, but I wasn't breathing rank horse pee.

Not that the air was much fresher when we reached Pethbridge's warehouse, for Doctor Bead had been here as well, giving his learned advice for cleansing away noxious gases by burning incense and camphor. The air was so thick with the fumes we'd more likely choke to death.

"Now what do you say?" declared Pethbridge.

He had set his wares out on display on a table under the window, and now he got down to business, unrolling his bolts of fine silk, French velvets and Florentine lace.

My father's brows were twitching. He was wearing his usual black coat. He claimed not to have any eye for judging such 'intricate fabrics'. And Pethbridge, shrewd as he was, turned all his attentions on Mother, craftily guiding her hand onto one of the costliest fabrics, letting her stroke and caress it.

"Magnificent – truly exquisite!"

"You might like to take it away... as a sample to view at your leisure? In fact, my dear Mrs Hopgood, as your husband and I will be partners, I'd like to offer it to you as a gift, for your own satisfaction."

"Make some dining room curtains," grumbled Father.

"My dear good sir," gasped Pethbridge, "this fabric's in vogue at Versailles, as worn by the Queen of France. Surely you'd like your own beautiful wife to look as divine in her prime, when she graces your table at dinner?"

Mother ought to have blushed with shame under her white lead, and she tried deflecting his words by telling him not to flatter. "You must know I'm far too old for such jests. You just need to look at my daughter. Why, Rachel will soon be old enough… to grace another man's table… should she be so lucky to find such a prosperous fellow as… you know what I mean, Mr Pethbridge."

Pethbridge gave her a look of sheer horror.

I tried to swallow a giggle and broke into a choking fit, brought on by the incense and camphor. By the time I'd been soothed with mulled wine, Father and Pethbridge were shaking hands. I realized they'd reached an agreement.

"Forty rolls of assorted fine fabrics," Pethbridge declared with a smirk. "Entirely yours, Mr Hopgood, as soon as you choose to collect them."

Chapter Four

August was bad, bad, bad.

In the first two weeks, the death toll per week doubled to more than 3,000, which meant 500 a day were dying of plague in the City. Father tried keeping this from me. He tried keeping me shut in the house. He went out every morning after making it clear to both Mother and I that neither of us were even to open the door and say hello to a stranger, for fear they would pass on disease.

So what I knew of the City during this plague-ridden month was all second hand from Jess, who got her information, more often than not, from her brother.

One thing I knew for myself was the smell of smouldering rags. These had been stuffed into braziers at the junctions of every throughway to ward off the pestilent vapours. The air in London was foul all the time, though usually worse in the winter, thanks to the sea coal we burnt in our hearths. But there was a muddle of other vile stinks. They leaked out from the heaps of skin and flesh piled up in knackers' yards, stinking blood and waste from the butchers', heads and scales from the fishmongers' stalls. And then, within half a mile of our house, there were leather tanners and dyers, soap boilers and makers of glue boiling up fat and bones. And lime kilns over the river puffing great clouds of white smoke that made your eyes sting and your nose run. But usually in the summer, a breeze would clear the air, blowing the clouds away.

Not this year. The air was stagnant, heavy and sticky with heat, so worn-out it made you breathless.

We had to stop going to church. My parents refused to say why. Jess told me the churchyards had been so dug up, the bodies were buried three deep, and lime had been spread on the ground like thick snow to try to cover the stench.

Rumours were going about that pits were being dug outside the City walls to make graves for thousands more, as if there would be no end until everybody was dead.

And the Mayor passed a new decree restraining all victims of plague, as well as those sharing their houses, from going out onto the streets except after 9 p.m., when all those still uninfected were put under general curfew.

"It won't be obeyed," Jess scoffed.

I just wished we'd left in July, before Father signed up with Pethbridge.

Mother's sister had written again, inviting us to

stay, though also to ask again if we had any further news about her dear son, Robert. But Father still hesitated about whether to close the warehouse, afraid if he fetched his new fabrics they'd be looted while we were away. Yet if we all stayed and we died here, I said, what use would our business be then?

Mother countered that, just as likely, we'd have our throats cut on the journey by one of the cowardly thieves who'd fled their haunts in the City to ply their trade safe from plague. Though as she pointed out, the news from Salisbury was far from good, with one of the Kings own grooms having contracted the plague, forcing the Court to move on yet again, this time to the town of Milton. This proved there was plague in the countryside too. Though not in Saxton, as yet.

So we took Dr Bead's Universal Pills – which gave us all diarrhoea – chewed cloves and drank mulled wine. We grated nutmeg on every dish. This offered the best protection, or so it was generally claimed, against catching plague from your dinner. But nutmeg was costly and in short supply because of the war with the Dutch. Father said they had the monopoly on shipping it from the East Indies. This was partly what the war was about.

And then, as if we didn't have enough to worry

about, Pethbridge turned up at our house. He begged to inform my father he had made the most dreadful mistake. "I need that bolt of Versailles back."

"But you gave it to me," explained Mother, widening her eyes in that playful way that must have looked charming... once.

"No, I don't think I made myself clear." Pethbridge would not meet her gaze. "I only meant to *lend* it to you, so you could have the pleasure of admiring it in your own home. But the fact is, I must have it back now."

Well, Father would have agreed, I think. He'd never much liked the pattern, or any cloth bearing a pattern. But Mother was not to be shifted.

She said, "Well, that's all very well, but wriggle as much as you like, you *gave* it to me, Mr Pethbridge, before we agreed to our business. And I have just wrote to my sister and pledged her four yards for some cushions. Not that she wouldn't look fine in a gown, but her husband's a miserable man."

Pethbridge stared at her, blinking aghast.

Mother's gaze had gone shrewd again now.

"In that case, I'm not going to quibble. I certainly don't wish to cross you. I'll happily swap it, Madam, for another, whichever you'd like."

"But I like this one, Mr Pethbridge."

"Yes, yes, but the fact is, dear lady, my patron, you know, Lord Beastor... he's set his heart on that bolt of Versailles to make a most splendid waistcoat. He is adamant. He loves the weave and the thread."

Mother drew herself up to full height. She was short but she had a grand prow, like a galleon set at full sail. There was really no stopping her now.

Pethbridge wavered.

And then I remembered something Pethbridge had said on the day we went to his warehouse. The consignment had just arrived. "Excuse me," I said, "Mr Pethbridge, sir. But I don't quite understand when Lord Beastor actually saw it to know that he loved it so much. Because when we saw it, you told us that we were the first. Then we took it."

Pethbridge blushed so his pimples went purple. All he could do was splutter. "It's all a great muddle, you've got no idea. How I'm torn to please everybody."

"Muddle or not," replied Mother, as grand as the Queen of France, "you'll kindly ask Lord Beastor to have his waistcoat made out of some other of your fine fabrics. As a gentleman, I'm quite sure he'll bow to the whims of a lady."

And so it was left. Though when I told Jess, she said her brother confirmed it: His Lordship had sent

Pethbridge over, having been through the stock bolt by bolt, and noticed which one was missing. Beastor had been attending the King on the day the consignment arrived, so he couldn't have seen it before!

Jess glared at it, propped by her bed. Mother had got her to bring it upstairs, 'to keep it out of harm's way', as if she thought Pethbridge was going to sneak back and spirit it out of the house.

"Toby says this has happened before," she said, "him going through all the stock when it comes, as if he knows all about it."

"Who, Pethbridge?"

"No, Beastor, you mop-head."

"But why should Beastor, I mean, he's a Lord. He's an aristocrat, not a tradesman!"

"He brings Pethbridge all his French contacts. Toby thinks he's been lending him money."

"How strange."

"Also, Toby told me, you remember when Robert went missing – Beastor got in a blind fury that day. He told Pethbridge to sort something out or their dealings would be at an end! Apparently he reminded him, said the same thing again, about this bolt of fabric."

"*Something*? What do you mean, Jess?"

"Robert must have gone back to the warehouse and Beastor was there. Something happened, something must have got said. At any rate, Toby says, Beastor got so mad, he went and threatened Pethbridge. Got him to fetch Simon Slop. And afterwards, poor old Slop, he was never the same, says Toby."

I stared at her in amazement. "Slop again? Never the same? Is that why Pethbridge fired him?"

Jess shook her head. "How should I know?"

I wanted to give her a shake. How could she be so unbothered? "Why didn't you say this before, Jess?"

"I only just heard from my brother."

"Why didn't *he* say this before?"

Again Jess shook her head in that slow, careless, open way to show it was puzzling to her too. But Toby was that sort of brother, a boy who could hold something back, then tell it as if he assumed you probably knew it already.

"He's a pea-brain, a half-wit," I muttered. Then I made up my mind. "I must see him. You tell him to come here tomorrow."

Our chance came the following afternoon, when Mother had an appointment with her Italian plasterer to finalize his designs. I knew she'd be far too engrossed, laughing with Signor Giorgio, to notice Toby slip into the house.

Of course he arrived a bit late, slightly drunk.

But what he said still made sense. Just a shame he'd not said it before because he'd not thought it important.

It turned out that Simon Slop had been working at Pethbridge's warehouse, helping him move the stock, on that day Robert disappeared. He'd not been quite the same after that, as if he had a bad shock. And once I'd questioned Pethbridge about Slop finding the glasses, Slop had been told to go, though well paid off for his troubles.

"But why? What happened, Toby?"

"Simon never would say," Toby said. "But he was no happy chappy. I happen to know that much."

"Nor am I," I said. "I must tell Father."

When Father came home that evening, lamenting the heat and the pestilent air, he first had to put up with Mother pleading for extra money to satisfy her plasterer. She'd started off trying to bargain him down, 'work being so scarce in this plague time'. This led Signor Giorgio to counter by claiming his work should be worth more because he was risking his life by staying here working in London. "Another ten guineas he asks, John. Such emotional people, these foreigners."

"Ten guineas? My dear, don't you realize–" Father let out a sad sigh. There was no point in reasoning with Mother. "My dear, I have to tell you straight, the contract is off. That is final."

"You're not dealing with Mr Pethbridge?"

"I am talking about Signor Giorgio. As soon as I've closed up the warehouse, we shall be leaving for Saxton."

"In that case," Mother looked shrewd again, "what about Mr Pethbridge's scheme? Don't try to avoid me on this, John. You've still not collected his fabrics."

"He annoys me, continually asking about your wretched sample. Can't we give back his bolt of Versailles?"

"I told him before."

"Now he's saying, Lord Beastor actually wanted it to give to the Earl of Styx. It's not wise to start crossing such people."

"Nonsense, husband, I just won't believe it. Good heavens!" She sounded outraged. "Lord Beastor's uncle could buy enough bolts of Versailles to wrap round the globe if he pleased. We're taking that bolt for my sister. Why can't you stand up for yourself, and either collect those fabrics or ask for the money he owes you for all that cloth you've supplied him!"

"I'm going to!" Father said hotly. "In the morning, first thing! Now then, Rachel?"

I told him my problem would wait.

Chapter Five

Father left Mother in an excitable state, not sure if we should be packing to leave, or hiding the bolt of Versailles. One moment she expressed terror of being waylaid on our journey, of highwaymen giving her plague, the next trying to make up her mind what gifts she should take for her sister.

"Of course, we must take the whole bolt," she declared. "It's not just for Martha's cushions. The seamstress in Saxton will run up a gown for far less than we'd pay in London. Though, of course, we must take her some pattern books. She'll not have a clue about fashions!"

I moved across to the window. The only passers-by were muffled against contagion, dressed up as if for cold winter, although it was hot and oppressive. They went hurrying past, looking anxious. But there was one man on the corner, that same hooded figure in black. So this was no trick of the night-time, no ghostly shadow, but real. He was facing away down the street, as if watching Pethbridge's warehouse.

Next moment, Father was out in the street. He was striding along looking grim. The man shrank back in a doorway. Father passed him and reached our front door. I hurried to let him back in, but I waited for him to speak first.

"Wasted journey," he finally grumbled. "Pethbridge wasn't at home. But that arrogant fop, Lord Beastor, was there. He was waiting for Pethbridge too. So just to pass the time, I made a light remark about that so-called Versailles stuff your mother holds so dear, and he clear near bit my head off. Told me he wanted it back forthwith or I would rue the day!"

"In what way?"

"That's what I asked him. Tried to make light of it, Rachel. Then he came on all friendly. Got Toby to make us that ghastly new drink. 'Koffee', it's called. I can't like it. But while it was brewing away, Beastor claimed it had been his idea for Pethbridge to buy my cloth to send across to France, and he would get Pethbridge to buy a lot more if I could do him this favour. I said I'd do anything else he liked, but it's not up to me – it's my wife, and she's not for turning, I told him. So then he replied, all haughty again, that a man can't be ruled by a woman, not with his business at stake. And I asked what he meant. Then he told me he'd have to order Pethbridge to cancel all our arrangements. I won't be allowed his French fabrics. Well, hang! I wouldn't be talked to like that. It's all too absurd! It's outrageous!"

"So what did you tell him, Father?"

"I answered him straight – 'Keep your fabrics!' In fact, I said where he could shove 'em!" And then Father burst into laughter, only breaking off when Mother swung into the room.

"What's this about fabrics?" said Mother.

I saved him by changing the subject. "That man in black who you passed outside, you don't know who he is, Father?"

Father looked back at me blankly. "I've not got a clue who you mean, dear."

"He was only a few feet away, the only man there. He saw you; that's why he backed into the doorway."

We both moved across to the window, but of course there was nobody out there.

I had the room to myself that night, as Jess had gone away to visit her sick mother.

Not sick with the plague, Jess assured us.

My mother had made her swear it upon the Holy Bible before she bestowed her permission.

This was only a troublesome ague which kept her indoors, in her bed. It might even help to preserve her, keeping her out of contact with other infected bodies. (More effective than Doctor Bead's pills!)

At any rate I was lying in bed, wondering about

that figure hanging about in the street, doubting more than ever what I thought I'd seen with my own eyes.

I peered up at the shadowy ceiling. I could just about see the oak beams, black stripes against the rough plaster thanks to a hazy moon shining in through the open window.

It looked sickly yellow – plague yellow. I could hear rats scuttling about underneath the floorboards.

The air stank of festering sewage.

The cesspits were overflowing – the slopsmen had not been for weeks – while the gutters were piled high with horse dung, kitchen waste, human turds.

The woman who used to bring us fresh milk hadn't turned up for ten days. The bakery on the corner had recently closed its doors, the markets were half deserted. Was everyone dying of plague, or had they just fled the city?

The night was eerily quiet. How many weeks had passed since I'd heard those servant girls giggling through the thin wall? Though what was there left to giggle about?

Down below, a cart creaked by. I heard a bell tolling, a man calling out for people to bring out their dead.

I couldn't see much down below. The upper floors of our house stuck out, obscuring much of the roadway. But as he moved on down the street,

I saw the man's shadowy figure holding a flickering lantern. Its yellowy light beamed over the ribs of a mangy donkey pulling a heavy old cart. The cart itself was in shadow, so I was spared the sight of what I could guess was inside it.

Back in bed I lay half awake, trying to stop myself thinking... only to find myself caught in a dream where the man was the same hooded figure in black who seemed to be haunting our street. I imagined him turning his head, looking up at me at my window. He had no face, no eyes. Just the smooth white bone of his skull with yellow teeth grinning at me. As if the man was a phantom, a vile apparition of death. And just for a moment, I wondered if this could be a portent?

An omen.

I'd die of the plague...

I was lying there, sweating so much my nightgown stuck to my body, too scared to move or open my eyes, when... I heard my door creak open.

My bed was on the far side of the room. Jess's truckle bed was between us. How I wished she was there, but she wasn't. Instead someone else was inside my room, half visible in the dull gloom. No doubt about it – a man. I froze, unable to open my mouth, let alone try to confront him.

He came closer, round Jess's bed, only to suddenly stop. He bent down, fumbling about, as if something was caught on the bedspread. And suddenly this made him human.

I screamed at him.

He blundered back, bashing his knee on the low truckle bed, and went tumbling over it, cursing, only to haul himself back on his feet and go crashing out through the doorway and off down the stairs.

I stopped screaming.

Now Father was calling, "What is it?"

A thump. A loud yell.

I swung out of bed. With one foot to the floorboards, I was treading on something. I knew the man must have dropped it. I scooped it up and went off down the stairs.

On the first floor I found Father kneeling, clutching his thigh, groaning quietly.

As Mother peered out from their bedroom holding a lighted candle, I saw there was blood on his nightgown.

"The rogue had a knife. He lunged at me!"

"But what was he doing upstairs, John?"

I opened my hand to show Mother. It shone in the light of her candle, a splendid silver button.

44

"Well, who would have thought it," said Mother. "A gentleman thief; we were honoured!"

"Oh, Mother!" I rolled my eyes.

"Oh, youch," exclaimed father. "My leg."

"But what did he want?" I retorted. "You don't think I asked him up there?"

"Damn fellow got lost," mumbled Father. "Come on, please, and deal with my wound."

"I daresay he stole the button as well from some other fine, wealthy person," said Mother, still holding it close to the candle.

"These are terrible times," agreed Father, while I was washing his wound. "No one's safe in their beds from these ruffians. They've nothing to fear worse than plague now."

But surely an ordinary ruffian would have tried forcing the strong-box down in my father's study. He'd have swiped a few pewter plates. I checked. The front window was broken, but not one thing had been taken. So why had he climbed to the top of the house, where generally servants were sleeping?

I'd still have believed in my phantom. More likely than a fool of a thief getting confused in the darkness. Except for that *real* silver button.

For the rest of the night I lay wide awake, afraid that the thief might return.

In the morning I waited for Jess. She was late. Instead of being on hand to help with the laundry as usual, she didn't turn up until dinner. In fact I was clearing the plates when I heard her voice from the kitchen. I found her dazed; not answering Cook, who wanted to know where she'd been.

Instead she grasped my hand and led me out into the yard. "Oh, Rachel," she gasped, "I have had such a fright."

"I've had a fright too!"

She ignored this, except by shaking her head, as if I had failed to appreciate how serious was her own story.

"Very well then," I said, and she told me.

"My idiot brother Toby – he near got buried alive!"

I allowed this was quite a bad fright for the boy. "No doubt he'd been drinking again?"

"Yes, trying to drown his worries. He's been scared he was dying of plague because of a lump on his neck, so he got himself near oblivious at The Sun Tavern last night. The next bit he couldn't remember. He must have tried walking home, but he must have passed out on the way. The next he knew he'd been thrown in a cart. He couldn't move, couldn't breathe, he said, because of the weight of stuff on him. He thought they were sacks of grain at first, except for the stench,

46

like bad meat!"

"Oh, God, no," I gasped. "No, you don't mean...?"

Jess nodded, her eyes shut. "Dead bodies. He passed out, near suffocated. Next thing, two men were lifting him out. They were just about to give him the heave into the Kingsland death pit. He screamed out. The men let him drop. Must have thought a dead body had come back to life. So there he was, down in the pit, hands burning from all the lime they use to cover the bodies, him struggling to get himself out. And finally somebody lends him a hand, and guess who it is?"

I was blank.

She looked disappointed. "Try, Rachel."

"Why? How should I know?"

"Simon Slop. Turns out he was working there, Rachel!"

I stared at her, open-mouthed. "So what did he say?" I asked feebly.

Now Jess looked rather less cocky. "What did he say about what? Hold on. You don't really think, after all he'd been through, my brother was thinking of asking what Slop might remember of Robert?"

I stared at her fiercely. "The numbskull. All right, Jess, tell Toby from me... he's got to take us... tomorrow."

47

"Tomorrow? Where to?"

"To that plague pit. To find Simon Slop again, stupid. I want him to be here, outside the front door, when the church of St Clement's strikes ten."

"We can't do that. There's a curfew; your parents would never forgive me. It's more than my job's worth, Rachel."

"I'm going," I said. "You can help me or not."

She took a deep breath. "Right… I'll ask him."

"And one other thing," I said sternly. "Show Toby this silver button."

Chapter Six

Toby refused to take us.

After suffering such horrors the night before, he was in no mood to agree to go back there ever again, even when I offered to let Jess pawn my gold locket to pay him a fee for his troubles. When Jess accused him of being a coward, he complained he was not feeling well.

"So that's the end of that," said Jess, not sounding too downcast about it.

"The end of what?" I said sharply. "If he won't come, then the least he can do is give us directions to find it. So long as he can remember how he got home from the pit. Go on, Jess. Go back and tell him I want him to draw us a map. And remind him about that button."

By late that afternoon I had a rough plan and knew where we needed to go. At least I hoped I did, though never having ventured so far away from home by myself, I'd have to rely on Jess. She'd know the way to Houndsditch at least. She went there to see her sick mother. From there we could aim for old Bishop's Gate, then carry on through Shoreditch, to find our way out to the pit.

★ ★ ★

The evening went on forever.

With my parents finally tucked up in bed, we waited another hour until the clock of St Clements chimed the half hour after ten. Then we set off, barefooted, downstairs.

Every movement made such a creaking noise, I was sure that Father would hear us and come rushing out with his pistol to take on another intruder.

Or rather, our gentleman thief.

For Toby had confirmed it, just as I thought he would. That wretched silver button was engraved with Pethbridge's emblem – a hog at a trough.

"So what? That doesn't prove anything, Rachel. He's always losing them," Jess said, while counting the minutes to leave. "You don't really think, with him coining it in, getting so rich as a draper, he'd take up a part-time hobby, breaking into folks' houses at night and stabbing 'em when they don't like it?"

"He wanted the bolt of Versailles back!"

"Oh, stuff and nonsense, Rachel."

"I'm going to challenge him!"

"Really?" She seemed to reflect for a moment. "Well, all I can say to that is, we've got enough trouble to get through tonight without storing more for the morning. Wait and see what you think in the clear light of day, if we're still alive. Cross your fingers."

We reached the ground floor, and I found the door key on its usual hook in the study. There wasn't another way out of the house, for the rear yard had walls all around it. Jess slipped the bolt, I turned the key, and we were outside in the street. I suddenly felt free as air.

The feeling did not last long. We ducked across Gracechurch Street, under Pethbridge's creaking signboard, and turned off by The Sun Tavern. The market was buried in shadows, deserted except for stray dogs picking over the leftover refuse.

Our shoes squelched deep in the sewage. It coated the hem of my gown. But that was a worry for later. Right now just the stench, and the rats in the mire, and shadowy figures ahead, were sufficient to fill me with horror.

A fire burnt in the open yard in front of the church of St Helens. Its fumes lay thick as a fog. Beyond it I heard people coughing. I wondered who they could be, out in the night, breaking curfew? From out of the haze I saw one, a most horrible apparition. An old man, his face raw with pustules. He was pulling another poor wretch by her legs, a woman in a thin petticoat, perhaps his wife or young daughter. Her face was too blackened and swollen to give any hint of her age. Her mouth lolled open wide although she was dead. Her head bumped along on the cobbles.

We crossed ourselves, hurrying past, holding our shawls to our faces.

I looked over the wall at the churchyard. And in the hazy moonlight I saw great heaps of earth. They were piled high either side of the pathway that led to the door of the church, so it looked like a sunken trench. All the grass and the gravestones were gone. In their place were just crude wooden crosses. And oh, the foul odour, like sour, rotting meat. But this was from people – not beasts.

I tried blurting out my feelings, but Jess cut me short with a hiss, tugging me on through an archway. We needed to keep ourselves 'level', she said, for fear of losing our way.

I realized how sheltered I'd been. The alley was less than three feet wide, with mean little rundown dwellings. They were crammed so close together there were doorways every three yards, half of them daubed with crosses.

We went through a covered passageway and emerged in a cramped, grimy court.

A single tree had grown there once, but now it was only a withered black stump with lines attached to hold washing. Beside it, a trough with a pump. Next to the trough was a cesspit. A thin white cat was eating a rat. One of the few surviving cats from the great cull, I supposed. But when it saw us, the cat bolted, leaving only the head and some gizzards.

I was too numb with fear to feel very scared any more. Though Jess was holding my hand so tight I couldn't have turned and run had a monster jumped out from a doorway, unless she was running like I was. But what was this?

Some way ahead, out on a wider throughway, I heard a slow grinding of thick wooden wheels biting into the unmade roadway. Then the faint clang of a hand bell. A voice hollered, over and over, getting steadily louder: "Lord have mercy. Bring out your dead."

With her fingers like claws, Jess dragged me back into a narrow stairwell. From here we looked out as the cart trundled past, nearly as wide as the alley. The cart was pulled by a heavy old horse. Her head was bowed, eyes unseeing, as if sleepwalking – or dead.

Then, thwack! I was struck in the face by something cold and damp. A putrid hand dangled over the side, the hand of a plague-ridden corpse. It left my cheek splattered and slimy.

I drew back in shock, my mouth open to scream. My throat was too constricted to let out any more than a gasp.

From the back of the cart I saw arms and legs,

grey-white but blistered and scabby. And heads lolling back, faces upside down, eyes bulging like rancid mushrooms. Very few of the bodies were clothed. Some were wrapped in grimy, stained sheets. Several were utterly naked.

"Come along." Jess tugged me forwards.

We bolted as fast as we could to get away from the nightmare. But as we emerged from the passage, I saw something worse: a child on the ground, his foot being gnawed at by dogs.

"Keep away. They might bite," Jess shouted, but I ran at them, swatting my hands left and right, screaming so loudly they reared back and went skulking into the night. The poor child lay limp in the gutter. I leant over him, squeezing his shoulder, asking if he could get up. But as his face flopped my way, his waxy lips peeled apart and his swollen insides burped out a great belch of a poisonous stink. In my haste to scramble backwards, I tumbled into the open drain.

On we went, my skirts now sodden, my left arm covered in filth. I was shaking with shock. I kept looking down, trying to concentrate on the ground in front of my feet. I felt I was sleepwalking now. It was Jess who kept us on course.

We walked across Spitalfields. Poor wretches

camped out in the open here, some healthy, some sickening and dying. We could hear coughing and groaning. But we were as shadows ourselves now, mingling in with the throng.

We came to Bishopsgate Street. Along here, flares were burning in brackets attached to the walls. Watchmen in masks, wrapped in cloaks, stood feeding a giant brazier with charcoal and pellets of camphor. One called out a leery greeting. But Jess tugged my hand, hissed, "Ignore them!" And we ran for it on down the street.

The City stretched further than I had supposed, with whole streets of fine new houses built out of brick and slate. But soon there were gaps between them with half-constructed houses. Then wide-open, desolate spaces with brick piles and timberyards. A giant ash pit, a foundry and ramshackle wooden enclosures for penning the beasts while they waited to make the last leg of their journey from farms far away in the countryside to the butchers inside the City. Though just slightly further on, as if passing heaven from hell, we found ourselves in a patchwork of vegetable plots and orchards with beanpoles and apple trees ghostly in the darkness against a hazy night sky. Our footsteps on the gravel excited grunts from a sty. Poultry clucked in their coups, and once a tawny owl came swooping low overhead.

I was wondering how we could tell if we were still on the right road, when a cart came trundling behind us. The driver was swathed in a shawl. I called to him, asking politely if this road would take us to Kingsland.

He let forth a torrent of curses, whipping his horse extra sharp, as if he couldn't believe we were asking an innocent question. As if no honest person would be on this road, not at this time of the night, only thieves – or the ghosts of dead girls.

The cart went past, heaped with bodies.

"We won't get lost now if we follow the stink," said Jess in a fake jaunty tone.

The road continued straight north.

Ahead, but off to the left, flares blazed in an open field.

The moon was behind a cloud now, and figures loomed out of the gloom; some with picks and shovels, others with horses and carts. The drivers were hooded, some wearing masks, others puffing away on clay pipes to keep the vile odours at bay.

We had to slip between them to reach the gate into the field. Nobody took any notice. The flares cast eerie shadows, sending up yellow sparks. In their light I could see a diagonal gash stretching from corner to corner; a deep oblong hole about two yards in width, with earth piled high either side.

And then I beheld other figures flitting about the field. Old women and girls like us, even a couple of boys no more then ten years old. Mourners or else, more likely, thieves come to pick over corpses, hoping for rings on the fingers, or even wrench out some gold teeth.

As to the burial pit, one end was piled high with bodies. They must have been five or six deep. Hundreds of them lay widthways, dumped on their bellies or backs. A few of them hunched on their sides, with arms or legs doubled over. There was even a body without any legs, the torso in a bad state, as if it had rotted and fallen apart before it had been picked up. Its features were battered and shapeless, but from the strong shoulders and tousled black hair I guessed this had been a young man. And into my head crept a thought: it might have been Robert down there.

I stumbled; I fell on my knees and might have tried mouthing a prayer, but couldn't make any sound. I didn't know what I was thinking. But Jess was clutching my shoulders, twisting away. She was puking.

And then a man was beside us, growling we shouldn't be here, young lasses like us. "You ain't going to find loved ones here. Their souls be departed, and lucky for them. Much better for you to go home, girls."

I managed to draw myself up. The fellow was shorter than I. His face was grimy, his hair a wild mess, yet his voice had not been unfriendly.

"Who are you?" I asked.

"Just one of the gang who's stupid enough to work here doing this digging and dumping. You don't want to know."

"But I do though."

I hurriedly took out some coins, while Jess broke in to tell him that her brother had been here the previous night. "He was darn near buried alive, sir. Simon Slop pulled him out of the pit. You know him, I think, as he works here. We came here so we could thank him. And we would thank you, if you find him."

His grin opened, showing black teeth. But then he was turning away, shaking his mop of dark hair. "What else though?"

The man wasn't stupid. As if we'd have come to this hellish place, at this time of night, to say thank you! I said we had something to ask him, for which I would pay a good price, "about another friend that he knew, a friend of us both who's gone missing."

The man weighed this up. "Well, I never, you share friends with Slop. A small world, eh? You'd find him down there, and good luck, lass."

A heavy hand gestured vaguely towards the end of the pit.

I saw a man knee-deep in bodies. He had his back turned to us still. He was shovelling white lime from a heap at the edge, sending up clouds of lime dust that had coated his hair, skin and clothes, making him look like a ghost.

Jess and I both called at once.

The man turned. His long thin face was white except for his eyes, glinting like watery diamonds in the light from those flickering flares.

I turned back to the man by my side. "That's not him."

He let out a dark little chuckle. "I didn't mean him that's standing. I meant him what's under his boots. Not that poor Slop's near the top any more."

I stared at him not understanding.

"Slop's dead of the plague, you dim hussy. He was stricken last night, gone first thing."

"You just mind your tongue!" Jess scalded.

But his words didn't seem that important, not now, surrounded by so much death.

The second man climbed from the pit. His lime-stained hand touched my knee. He managed to heave himself upright. "I'm sorry, don't mind my friend here. I got on well with young Simon. He told me

59

some things. I could share them?"

I nodded.

He looked uncertain. "My wife died of plague last July. I've got six young mouths that need feeding…"

I showed him my open purse.

He emptied it out, then went on. "It was when he fell ill Simon told me. As if something weighed hard on his conscience."

"*Something?*"

"He just followed instructions, never knew what they were planning. Thought he'd been told the truth – that the young man's sweetheart was waiting, wanting to see him, in secret. Behind The Sun Tavern, they said. So Simon did that, in good faith. Then saw how they grabbed him and dragged him away. They had a boat waiting for him."

"*They?*"

"Don't know who they were, miss, but Simon guessed who must have hired them."

"And who would that be?"

"His employer, of course. But only because his employer was put up to it, by Lord Beastor. Or leastways, that's what *he* said."

Chapter Seven

In the morning I was intending to go and tell Father.

Jess stopped me. She said he would never believe we'd even been to the plague pit, let alone met a man who'd be scrupulous, restricting himself to the truth when he'd got his eye on my purse. "Your dress could have got in a state like that just by crossing the street," she insisted.

"Very well. Then we'll have to go across and challenge Pethbridge directly, ourselves!"

Jess pointed out this was hopeless. "He'd laugh in our faces, you silly!"

"Not if we called in the constable."

"We'd have to persuade the constable first. We'd have to know why it all happened."

Well, what I still didn't know, and what I wanted to know, was *why* they had got rid of Robert. Had they done it from personal spite or to cover up some other evil? Had Robert overheard something? And how might it link with their desperate need to get back that bolt of Versailles?

"Most likely it doesn't," said Jess.

Perhaps I was crazy to care. But all I could think about was poor Robert, thrown in the river.

Drowned, washed away downstream. Though with so many dead of the plague, why should Robert's death matter so much?

It had mattered to Simon Slop. I thought it would matter to Father, especially now Beastor had riled him. I made up my mind I would tell him the lot, whatever Jess thought of my chances. But not until she'd had the chance to talk with her brother again. Slop's tale might wake up some memories.

At dinner my father had plenty to say about us escaping the City. He had hired a carriage with horses to be in the street the next morning. "This is very short notice," said Mother.

"I have only one thing to sort out, dear. A short letter to write to Pethbridge."

"Why can't you meet him in person?"

"My dear, I have done my best several times, but Pethbridge appears to be absent."

"So what would you tell him, John? Apart from presenting a final demand for the cloth you supplied in good faith, and asking him, please, will he pay you?"

Father said this needn't concern her, not now, which brought on a stormy reaction about falling out with Lord Beastor.

A while later he drew me aside with a stern look

on his face, as if he had heard of my exploits.

The chance was too good to miss. I told him about the button belonging to Giles Pethbridge. I told him what Toby had said. But just when I was bracing myself to tell him about the plague pit, we heard Mother out in the corridor shouting at the top of her voice. "Where do you think you have been, Jess, skiving off work when there's packing to do?"

We both hurried out to hear more.

Jess seemed not to hear the question. Indeed, she looked so distracted she didn't see me in the doorway until I asked what was the matter, for there were tears on her cheeks, and Mother could never have brought those out. I knew Jess well enough!

She told me Pethbridge's house was shut up with all the servants gone, so no one had answered the door.

"But what about Toby?"

She sobbed out loud. "I heard muffled cries from up top. As if Toby was trying to call to me, but he wouldn't come to the window. I kept shouting. It was wide open. Then I just heard this dreadful, most terrible noise, like a dog being tortured it was."

"Load of rot." Mother put both her hands on her hips. "Excuses, excuses. We have work to do."

"No, Betsy," said Father. "Let's check this."

Taking Jess by the hand, I followed Father across the street.

We knocked and no one answered, though again we heard crying upstairs. So Father hurried back home to fetch our handyman, Joe. Joe came with a hammer and chisel. Then Father gave the order, and Joe assaulted the shutters that closed off the ground floor shopfront.

A few blows, the shutters crashed back. We stepped into an empty shop.

The 'finest fabrics' had been packed away. The door to the hallway was locked.

Again Joe wielded his hammer, and all of us hurried upstairs.

Pethbridge's house was wider than ours. His main parlour was on the first floor, with a dining room to one side and sleeping quarters above, all furnished in the most opulent style within the last few years, so very much *à la mode*. There were glass chandeliers, painted panels and the most intricate hangings, with a couple of carved oak dressers loaded with pewter and silverware, and fine blue china from Delft. Enough to make my mother green with hopeless envy.

The third floor was far less ornate though, this being just for the servants. It was only an attic, with low tilting beams divided by wooden partitions. And from the far end came more crying, with whimpering, groans and gasps.

Father called out, "May we enter?"

Jess didn't wait for an answer. Sweeping aside the cloth hanging draped across the entry, she barged through with me close behind.

And oh, what a sight met our eyes.

If last night had been like a vision of hell, what was this but with greater refinement?

For Toby was stretched on his narrow cot bed, naked except for a sheet drawn across his middle.

Straps were attached to his ankles and wrists, holding him tight in place.

Leaning over him, like a vile monster about to devour its prey, was a man with a hideous mask on his face. A mask with a great wooden beak. Its nostrils were puffing out smoke. The smoke reeked of incense and camphor. His hands were encased in black gauntlets pressing down on two glass jars either side of Toby's neck. They were hot and steamy inside, forcing the flesh into bumps. And each jar contained several hornets. These were buzzing dementedly round, pinging against the glass and tumbling down onto the swellings, which were dripping with gingery pus.

Toby screamed. His whole body convulsed. The hornets were stinging his wounds.

"What's the meaning of this?" cried my father.

The figure backed off. By the window, its hands reached to lift off the mask.

"Dr Bead," I gasped.

He almost smiled. His plump face was deathly pale, except for the vivid red marks on his cheeks where the mask had dug into his skin. "Keep away if you value your lives, my good friends. The patient is sorely afflicted."

"You're torturing him," Jess shouted.

"I have purged him and bled him, but to no avail. You see those swellings – plague buboes – they're full of vile pus," said the doctor. "If we leave them, the pus will kill him. That is why I'm experimenting, aggravating the buboes. When they are full, I'll remove them, applying hot tongs and a blade. If the treatment should work, and there is a small chance, I can try it on fee-paying patients. So stand back please. I have every right. Mr Pethbridge has given *carte blanche*."

"Why, where is he now? Where's Lord Beastor?"

Bead blinked as if he'd not seen me before. "Out of the City, of course. They are wisely biding their time until this affliction is over."

Then Toby yelled yet again.

I feared the hornets had stung him, but this time it was his sister. She prized both jars from his neck, releasing the angry insects. They buzzed round in frantic circles, banging into the walls. One of them swooped so low it got tangled up in my hair.

Father managed to flick it away. It buzzed into Bead. The man swotted his nose. It stung him. He yelped with the pain. Then the doctor was up on his feet, flapping his arms in the air. But by then all the hornets were gone, flown out of the open window.

The room was suddenly quiet.

"Now you get out too," said Jess.

She picked up his wooden mask and chucked it hard at his chest. It bounced off and hit the floor, splitting in two. "Listen well. If you bother my brother again, I'll kill you, I promise you that. With your hot tongs," said Jess. "I'll have your *carte blanche* from the devil-in-chief. And I won't be charging a fee."

Dr Bead flapped his lips in shocked horror, glancing across to my father, as if seeking some adult support. But Father just glared at him sternly.

"You'll regret this," Bead muttered, "you ignorant fools."

Then, snatching his jars and his carrying case, he was gone without further remonstrance, clattering off down the stairs.

My father took a deep breath, his eyebrows twitching. "Oh, dear. We must find you another doctor."

"No, thank you, sir," said Jess. "I'll tend him until he gets well. It's calm and rest that he needs from now on. Not any more doctors' treatments."

Jess wouldn't change her mind about this. Father said he would send food and drink, candles, fresh towels and bedding, to try to make both of them comfy.

Mother was cross when she heard. The linen and towels would be ruined, she said. They'd have to be thrown away or burnt to get rid of the plague germs. "Such extravagance just for mere servants!" And she was even more grieved when she realized our travel plans would have to be changed, postponed until Jess could come with us.

I wanted to know how she was, but Father would not let me back there again. He insisted I stay in our house, 'out of harm's way', so he said, until we set off for the country.

We were at home Sunday morning when Jess came into the parlour. Her face was white and drawn, her eyes red. She talked without moving her lips.

"As if he was suffocating," she said. "Like drowning, his lungs full of fluids. It took him all night, but he's gone now. My Toby's at peace, and God bless him."

We all gathered round, even Mother. We all did our best to console her.

But then Jess drew back. "Sorry, sorry–" and cupping her hand to her mouth, she sneezed, and she sneezed again.

"Poor girl's caught a cold," exclaimed Mother. "She needs a rest. Put her to bed."

Chapter Eight

It happened alarmingly quickly.

Before the clocks struck midday, Jess was in bed, very sick.

She ought to have had my bed, but Mother would not allow this. She insisted Robert's things should be cleared so Jess's truckle bed could be brought downstairs and set up in the lobby just behind Father's office. She had tapers burning to clear the air between that hole and the hallway.

I was instructed to keep well away.

I only agreed to this because I still wanted to think Jess had a mere passing fever, a reaction to what she'd been through, and what she most needed was peace and calm. Though I had no choice in the matter. The door was kept locked. Only Cook was allowed to go in and tend to my friend.

Meanwhile, Mother got very worried about her bolt of Versailles because it had been in our room.

"But why should that matter?" asked Father, as we sat down to our supper.

"Well, if the girl carries contagion, supposing the fabric's absorbed some of her vapours? It might give them off, and poor Rachel might end up breathing them in? In which case it might have been better to give it straight back to its owner."

"You are its owner now, dear."

"But what should we do? Should we burn it? I can't bear the thought."

Father reasoned that this was uncalled for. "The girl didn't sleep in her bed last night, and it is a well-known fact, the pestilence wastes no time, dear."

Which was lucky for me, I supposed. The fabric stayed in my room, wrapped in an old cloth sack.

I sat up there alone all evening. I was worrying how this would end. Supposing, God preserve us, Jess *had* contracted the plague, I couldn't face the thought that I might lose my best friend.

I heard the death cart go by.

I looked out and saw poor Toby's limp corpse bundled up in a blanket, being carried from Pethbridge's house. And as the cart trundled on, I looked down and saw the bare body, tangled with four or five others, on its last ride to the plague pit.

I drew back in horror. A vision of death!

I went to bed. Half asleep, I heard my bedroom door open. The shadowy form in the doorway made me think of that hooded man before I remembered the thief, and then I was blurting, "No, spare me. Whoever you are. Leave me be."

Then I heard Father's soothing voice. I sat up with

a start. He was standing there in the doorway, his hand cupped round a candle so the flame lit up his face from below.

The sight was strangely soothing.

I asked him how Jess was doing.

Father said she'd been talking but not making sense, "…about going up to Kingsland. She says you'll be taking her *back* there, as if you've both been there already!"

I nearly spoke out. One more second I would have told him our secret; how we had foolishly risked our lives by making that trek to the death pit. Instead I was saved by a knock on the door, a voice from out in the passage.

It was Cook, the dear, kind woman. Her long, grey hair was let down for the night; she was wearing a plain, linen nightgown. She blurted that would we forgive her coming intruding like this, but she thought we should know, "Poor Jessie, she's fighting for breath, sir. It's vile to behold. I can't help her, not by myself, sir."

"I'll be straight down," said Father.

I rushed after them both down the stairs.

My dear friend was sitting up in the bed, leaning forwards, clasping a bucket. Her hair was in greasy tangles, her nightgown stuck to her body, her tired face mottled and glistening. Her eyes were enormous, rimmed with mauve as if they were badly bruised. But worse, her neck was distorted. It was all swollen up round the sides, under her ears, like ripe apples.

Buboes.

Our eyes met for a split second. I think she mouthed my name. Then Father was shouting, "In God's name, foolish girl, what are you doing here, Rachel? Don't breathe in the air, here. Please, leave us."

But I stuck my ground. I would not back out.

Instead I pushed even closer, falling down on my knees by the bed, grasping my friend by the hand. Her palm was hot, slimy wet. I held it up to my cheek.

"You'll get better soon, Jess. I know it. Don't answer me. Save your breath now."

Instead she was coughing again, coughing out phlegm streaked with blood. And then she retched into the bucket again.

And so it went on all night.

Sufficient to say, she was gone from this world before the first light of dawn.

My only best friend was... *at peace?*

In fact I thought it shameful, the haste with which my parents insisted the body should be removed.

Jess was out of our house before her body was cold. This was largely thanks to my mother. For someone had told her, when death intervened, the pestilential vapours oozed quickly out from the corpse to find a new host to devour.

Father paid those who took her away to treat her with all due dignity, though no clergyman could be found to say a prayer at her passing. Our own vicar had died two weeks back. And no one she'd known could accompany her on her last journey – to Kingsland.

We ate in the kitchen that morning, Cook and ourselves, sharing bacon and bread. Though none of us did more than pick at the food. Mother and Father kept murmuring on over what course of action to follow.

We had lost another day, but Mother could see no reason why we should not leave on Tuesday. Father had to point out, with a death in the house, we would need clean bills of health to legally start on our journey.

Mother dismissed this as typical, her husband a weak, cautious fool. "As if in these times folk who value their lives take heed of such petty fogging!"

"You want us sent back?" Father wanted to know, in his mildest, most reasonable tone. "Besides, this shouldn't delay us much, dear, if I go and see Bead this morning. I'm sure for a generous fee he'll sort out our papers in no time."

I wondered if Bead would forgive us for the way he'd been driven away.

I even wondered, just briefly, if maybe his awful treatment might have saved Toby's life, and then Jess might have lived too? For what did we know about plague?

Perhaps I was also infected? Then Father and Mother would catch it? How long had Jess been infected before she'd been taken ill? Supposing that Toby had caught it from tumbling into the plague pit, had she picked it up the next morning? Or had she not contracted it until we both went back that night? In that case her death might be my fault. We had taken a terrible risk.

I went off upstairs, trying to pray to God that we would all be spared. But my mind was seething with worries that took my attention from God. Besides, He had shown no mercy to all those other poor souls. Why should He care to spare me?

As for Dr Bead, he wasn't at his apothecary's shop when Father called to see him. Father had to go and seek him at the local tavern. He found him devouring roast beefsteaks and ended up footing the bill. After which the doctor told him that there could be no question at all of us having clean bills of health. "How could I grant such passports, dear sir, when contagion is rife in your house?"

"Rife in our house?" gasped my father. "What nonsense. Its victim is dead!"

"Death makes matters worse, my dear sir. For it would be most unusual for one death to lead to no others. This last week a thousand have died every day. Yet you have the bare-faced impudence to come to this public place breathing your noxious vapours over these innocent people? Have you no shame? Stay at home, sir. Rules are for everyone, rich and poor. We can't make exceptions for drapers."

Of course, Bead was getting his own back. But he had the law on his side. No sum of money would change his mind. Father came home expressionless. We sat down to a gloomy dinner.

"It has come to this – we are prisoners in our own house," whimpered Mother, after wasting a great deal of breath reminding us of our stupid mistake in nursing a servant girl. "Now we're all going to die in this place."

I tried to cheer them up by reminding them nothing had changed. We might not have got clean bills of health, but there was still nothing to stop us from slipping away out of London. Pethbridge had done the same thing, leaving his house infected with Toby still on his death-bed, and Bead had done nothing to stop him!

Father got up and moved to the window, as if not sure what to do nor where his duty lay. I saw his expression alter from baffled concern to surprise as he peered through the glass. "Who's that fellow?"

I joined him, half afraid it might be that figure in black, though part of me hoping it was, for if he'd been seen by Father as well, it meant I wasn't alone in conjuring such a phantom.

But this man was short and stocky. He was wearing a grey sort of uniform with a three-cornered hat. He was standing on our front doorstep, leaning on a stout cudgel. In his left hand he held a rolled scroll.

Father went out to ask what he wanted.

When Father returned he looked grave. No, more than that – he looked angry. His dear, honest face was livid, brow trembling, eyes like jellies.

"What's the matter?" my mother demanded.

"The doctor reported us, Betsy. Now the constable's sent a watchman to stop any comings or goings except by his special permission. He demanded I give him the key! He says if we need food and drink, he will have them sent in for a fee."

Mother fell back in her chair, pressing her hands to her face, while under her breath she was talking to me: "I should never have married your father."

Not that Father was listening. "We will not be prisoners," he stated. "We'll leave here one way or another."

"In winding sheets," Mother countered.

Father's silence seemed to suggest he still had to think of a plan.

The backyard had no way out. Our own front door was locked. And if we climbed out of a window, the watchman was sure to spot us. Father's words seemed horribly hollow.

So was Mother right? We were stuck here until death set us free?

It came to me not long after, while I was up in my room. I was feeling so quiet, alone there, with dear Jess gone forever. I remembered us giggling together. Then remembered those servant girls who worked for Widow Blunket, giggling on the far side of the wall. Not any more. All quiet.

That's what gave me my clever idea. That there might be another way out after all, if we had the strength to make one.

I went back downstairs to tell Father. "We'll need that hammer and chisel," I said. "We're going to need Joe to help us."

"Do what?"

"Come upstairs quickly and I'll show you."

Chapter Nine

We started work that evening, trying to do it quietly for fear the watchman would hear.

My plan was simple enough.

Father confirmed that down below the partition wall was of brick, whereas up here, in the attic, the wall was of wattle and daub.

Cook and her husband Joe both agreed, old Widow Blunket had not been seen over these last few weeks, so no doubt she'd fled the City, leaving her dwelling closed up.

Her quarters were on the two upper floors, with her own outside stairs at the rear, leading down to her own small yard. It was blessed with a gate to a passageway opening out onto Clements Lane.

Joe didn't take long to hack his way through the first outer skin of the wall. This was made up of lime and horsehair. He soon found a vertical joist to which the wattle was nailed. He managed to break some away. Behind was a two-inch gap, then another layer of wattle, thickly plastered on the far side.

It took Joe a couple more hours to make a hole big enough for Mother to climb through with ease. Meanwhile, we got on with the task of whittling down our baggage to what we could carry by hand.

Father thought it far too risky to try to send a message arranging for the carriage-man to meet us in the morning, even some way away from our house. We'd have had to rely on the watchman to find a delivery boy, and the watchman would probably read it.

Instead we would have to leave London on foot. Though if we could walk to Whitechapel, Father thought we might hire a coach from the inn that was on the High Street.

Mother was most put out. She said she could never manage without her whole chest of clothing, and what about her bolt of Versailles that she'd fought so hard to hold onto? "It comes, or I don't. And that's final."

So in the end Joe agreed to come, with a handcart from nextdoor's yard.

The clocks had struck eleven when Joe lugged the chest through the hole. And while I was helping Mother squeeze through, he went on down the stairs to open the door to the yard, prepared to smash it if need be.

The servant girls' room was smaller than mine. It had a great trough of a bed and a rough wooden box in the corner. This was covered with so much dust, I reckoned the room had been empty at least since the end of July. But as I was pointing this out, we heard such a bellow from down below, I knocked the candle over.

Father raised a hand to stop Mother, but of course I followed behind him downstairs to the floor below.

Joe was in the large room at the back, fingers pegged to his nostrils. The stench was nauseating. He said the door had been closed, but he'd smelt something bad from the passage. Nothing could have prepared him, or me, for what we beheld in that room.

The air was soon seething with blowflies woken up by the light of our candles. And in the bed, Widow Blunket lay propped with bolsters, as if she'd been waiting to greet us.

Her face was like leathery parchment. It was gnawed away on one side, exposing chalky white bones and a grin made of crooked brown teeth.

In the corner a dog was curled up, as if it was still fast asleep, but its fur was falling away, exposing its ribs and dried innards.

Two victims of plague in one room.

"We must leave this," said Father softly. "Close the door, don't tell your mother. And if she questions the smell, say meats have gone bad in the kitchen."

Within five minutes or so we were out in Clements Lane. We made good progress the next

81

quarter hour, finding our way through dark alleys and courts along the north side of Eastcheap. But then the inevitable happened.

We came out in a small cobbled square with an old brick well in the middle. By the well was a heap of bodies stacked very neatly like logs, and part covered up with some sacking so we couldn't see their heads. But it was too much for Mother. She sank down on the cobbles as if kneeling to pray.

"God bless us, she's fainted," said Father.

We tried but could not revive her. Instead I had to carry two bags, Father carried the bolt of Versailles, and Joe had to push the handcart with Mother on top of her clothes chest, her face down, arms and legs either side.

Like this we continued eastwards. We kept south of Fenchurch Street, coming out by the church of St Catherine, where a giant bonfire was burning. At first I thought it to be a great pyre, that now they were *burning* the dead. But instead it was only bundles of clothes, bedding and other fabrics stripped from plague victims' houses. Or so at least Joe suggested.

In the light of these flames we were spotted. Three men stepped out from the churchyard. One of them held up a lantern, the other two pointed their muskets.

I feared they were robbers at first, until I saw their brass badges and realized they were night watchmen, wanting to know our business and why we were breaking the curfew.

None of us answered. What could we say? I felt sure we'd be escorted back. Then the man with the lantern moved closer, frowning down at Mother who still lay slumped on the handcart.

"God rest her soul," the man sighed. "If you carry on, sir, where Fenchurch meets up with Leadenhall Street, there's a pile of dead waiting collection."

So on we went, out of Aldgate and along towards Whitechapel. We found the inn on the High Street and thought our troubles were over.

Alas, they had just begun.

The inn was shut for the night.

Father woke up a solitary hostler who told us, none too kindly, they had no horses here or even a room for the night. Joe thought we'd do well to continue up towards Bethnal Green.

So we carried on. We followed dark empty byways, leaving the houses behind. But the road was too bumpy and Mother woke up, and in the end we decided to get some rest under a hedge.

When dawn broke we were so cold and so stiff,

we wanted to move on at once just to try to get warm. However, we soon lost our way.

We ended up in Hackney, a pleasant enough little village, a little before midday. And here, at last, we struck lucky. A passing clergyman directed us to the house of a poor young widow. Her husband was recently dead of the plague. He had left her with five young children, as well as a horse and a haycart she didn't have any use for. Except to demand a high price.

After loading the cart, Joe bid us farewell. He had to get back to the house to take Cook away to Brixton, where her brother had a small farm. I only hoped we would meet them again. I felt sad seeing Joe go. But after that we made progress, travelling up the Lea Valley, coming out in a dense leafy forest. By the end of the afternoon, we were close to a village called Epping, and as we were all exhausted, we decided to stop for the night, setting up a sort of camp for ourselves under the wheels of the cart.

Next day we continued along a good road, only to find our way barred by townsmen manning a checkpoint. They said we could not enter Chelmsford unless we could vouch for our business.

We had to make a long detour down narrow, winding lanes.

However, we met an old farmer bringing his cows back to milk. He asked us to join him for supper, and as he was that fascinated to hear how the plague had gripped London, we ended up staying the night, sleeping in good linen sheets. Next morning we left with a good chicken pie to help us along on our journey.

Mother was queen of the cart, complaining of all the jolting, while Father led the horse by its rein with me tagging on at his side. My hair was soon dusty, my nose crusted up. My thin leather shoes gave me blisters, no match for the hard, rutted road.

"It gets worse when it rains," said Father. "I've heard of men drowning in potholes."

But we were alive – we were safe from the plague.

At least, I very much hoped so.

Chapter Ten

How many days to reach Saxton? I was past counting the days.

The dust had turned to a slimy sheen over my face and arms, and I was dreadfully tired. The shadows seemed to mirror my mood, tapering dense and black like tentacles from a sea monster, trying to wrap themselves round my legs to drag me into the hedgerow.

Exhaustion was making me mad.

A few miles away from the village, we came to a minor crossroad. Instead of a signpost pointing the way, there was a gallows post. A boy no older than Robert hung limp from a thick brown noose, his neck distended and twisted. His face was bloated and blackened. His eyes had been pecked by the crows.

Death couldn't shock me any more, not after all I had seen. But I turned away, making the sign of the cross. And that was when I saw him, across the neighbouring field. He was by the edge of a copse of trees – a figure in black staring at us.

I grasped at Father's arm, pointing across the field. But before I could get his attention, the figure had disappeared, melting back into the shadows.

"What is it, Rachel?"

I shook my head, too giddy with tiredness and

thirst to know quite what I had seen.

In fact I was almost relieved when Father changed the subject, waving his arm at a tower that was visible over the treetops.

"There now, the village of Saxton. Another quarter hour and we shall be safely arrived."

But on the approach to the village, we found our way blocked by two ruffians raising pitchforks at us. They said that their village was clean of the plague, and they were taking no risks letting strangers get closer. "Where are you from?"

"From London."

They were only young farm lads with smooth chins and spots. They hastily backed off from Father as if he was sent by the devil.

Mother stirred herself high in the cart. She looked a lot less stately than she would have liked, I was sure. And she'd have been badly shocked had she seen her own face in a mirror. It was caked with a thick mask of dirt, murky brown, with bloodshot holes for her eyes and a gash where her lips should have been. But she certainly shocked the two men, even before she announced loud and clear, in her most ominous tone, "I'm Martha Duncan's sister. Now let us through this instant or you will be made to regret it."

The two lads led the way into Saxton.

Chapter Eleven

Robert had described Saxton as 'a few huts built around a bog. They're all dolts and zealots that live there'.

And certainly at its centre there was nothing but open ground, with a few tethered goats and a cow. Humble hovels of wattle and timber bordered it on three sides, with the old church on its far side, along with a few good houses built of brick and tile.

Mother piped up, "Your aunt's house, dear, it's the one all covered in ivy."

The ivy grew over the rooftop. It certainly looked tumbledown, though its garden was well enough tended, with a huge vegetable plot leaving no space for weeds.

A lichgate led into the churchyard on the far side of the wall. And further on from the church were the old gates to Saxton Hall, all overgrown with brambles. The hall had been set on fire during the Civil War. I remembered Robert telling us the squire had been a staunch Royalist.

We left the cart in the lane and walked up the path to the house where Robert had lived for twelve years. But as Father reached for the bell chain, one of our new friends warned us we ought go round the back.

"Parson Duncan don't welcome disturbance, not when he's writing his sermons."

We knocked on the kitchen door.

The woman who let us in was nothing like I remembered. I hadn't seen my Aunt Martha since I was seven or eight, and if I'd grown up like she told me I had, she seemed to me to have shrunk. She was timid and tense, and her hair had gone grey, and her apron was white with flour from kneading some dough to make bread. But she bustled us into her kitchen, delighted to see us come safe.

It was good to wash our faces from a bowl brought in from the yard, then settle down at a table while Aunt heated up some thick soup. She told Father to pour himself ale.

And soon they were reminiscing about their last time together, when Aunt had come down to London. Late May in 1660, when King Charles had returned from France. All the church bells had chimed their greetings, and thousands had danced in the streets. And we were all feeling quite snug and at home when the door opened from a dark passageway, and in peered Parson Duncan.

He was short like his wife, but solid and strong. He had taut lips and coal-black eyes. I saw how he glared at his wife before seeing her guests sitting there. Then his whole expression arranged itself into a smooth good humour, and he came striding forwards to squeeze Father's hand and give Mother the sort of consoling embrace a good father might give his daughter. He even tried patting my forehead. "A dear, sweet, innocent girl."

And then he was saying how sorry he was, not having welcomed us at the front door. "But it is the Sabbath tomorrow. The Lord's work must always come first. You will worship with us in the morning, I trust?"

Father assured him we would. He said how grateful we were too, for granting us shelter at such a bad time, "though I'm sorry we bring no more news."

"News?" said the Parson. "Of what, sir?"

"Of your son."

"No cause to say more." Parson Duncan had a set look.

"But we miss him, as surely you do."

"No, sir. He was lost to the Lord on the day he left home for the City."

I glanced at my aunt. She looked down, her face pale.

"But… a good enough lad," blathered Father.

"He worked hard; he wasn't a wastrel."

Parson Duncan wiped his hands, and with his gaze to the ceiling, murmured that as we were here as his guests, we would kindly respect his judgment. "The boy had the devil within him."

There was an ice-cold silence.

Poor Robert, I thought. A stepfather like that, no wonder he'd fled to London! "Supposing he's dead?" I said carefully. "He did nothing bad that we know of. One shouldn't speak ill of the dead. And now we've got reason to worry because-"

"Rachel dearest..." Father was soothing. "You're tired from all our travelling."

"I have something to say!" I pleaded.

Parson Duncan cleared his throat, speaking over my head. "No doubt that's the way in the City, but here we expect our children to be meek and mild. And obedient."

"Yes, silence, Rachel," said Mother.

"But-"

"John, fetch the bolt of Versailles."

While Father meekly got up and went to unload the cart, she kept up a barrage of small talk about the new trade in fine fabrics brought specially over from France, and what was in vogue now at Court. My aunt glanced across at her husband. His gaze was still fixed on the ceiling, hands clasped, knuckles white on his lap. So we waited. Father came back.

"It's a bit of a mess on the outside."

The sack was splattered and grimy from so many days on the road.

"Unwind it, John. Show my sister."

Father dutifully took it out of the sack, but the fabric was filthy as well, with a ragged hole gnawed at one end. And then we found out the reason. A few shreds of paper fell out, and then a dead rat, shrivelled up as if it had been there for weeks.

"How most disappointing," gasped Mother. "Thank goodness I stopped you from getting involved and doing a deal with that Pethbridge! A mercy indeed."

"Yes, thanks be." Parson Duncan had a ratchet grin. "My wife has been spared from temptation. Such fancy stuff is the devil's own work and not welcome in *my* house. We make do with plain English cloths here."

Mother opened her eyes very wide, but rather than answering… she sneezed.

As to my room it was plain but clean. It was good to have space to myself. I lay on the hard, narrow bed thinking about where I was; in the house where

Robert had lived all those years, under his stepfather's thumb. For the first time I understood why Robert had been so desperate to get away from this place. And why he had been so scathing about his stepfather's 'religion'.

But I was so tired that I soon fell asleep. And when I next opened my eyes, the bedroom was bright with sunshine. Nearly time for our Sunday worship.

Chapter Twelve

All the villagers came to the service, except for three who were sick. I knew because Parson Duncan noticed and asked where they were.

The service was held in the old village church, though Parson Duncan's faith was more extreme than our local church. At home we prayed for His Majesty, our church full of flowers and incense. The walls here were crudely whitewashed, the old stone statues defaced.

I remembered Robert telling me, the Squire's brother had been the rector. When Cromwell's army had sacked the hall, the rector was shot in the churchyard.

I stirred to find Parson Duncan had got up to start his sermon. *It went on for an hour and a half.*

"Sodom and Gomorrah were destroyed by the wrath of the Lord, so London, with its evil ways, has been humbled by the Lord, the pestilence being His punishment. I say this will only end when all its sinners are rotting in hell, or else they repent in His mercy. And thus we are spared in this village, so long as we trust in the Lord and keep to His path. Let us pray now."

My knees had cramps from kneeling so long by the

time we were out of that church. We had been in there nearly three hours.

I stood in the sunshine outside the porch, unable to stifle a yawn. Then my aunt took my arm. "Dear Rachel, will you come for a walk with me, please. There is something I think I should tell you. Something I want you to know."

I followed her out of the lichgate and waited for her to speak, but she carried on walking in silence, as if she was leading me somewhere.

We reached the far side of the green, passing an old stone cross. Then carried on down the lane towards the spot where the yokels had stopped us the evening before. Two others were out there now, guarding their flimsy barricade, and as we approached they saluted. My aunt greeted both with their names.

"This way," she said, leading me off the track down a path that cut through some woodland. "Though we could sit on this stump if you like? My dear, you're looking so careworn."

I said that if she was willing, I'd like to continue our walk. I said I had something to tell her.

I wanted to talk about Robert, but had to start with the whole murky tale about Father's dealings with Pethbridge. This led me back to Lord Beastor, and Simon Slop's part in the plot.

"Ah, yes... I felt it last night," she said. "You were fond of my boy; you cared for him?"

I nodded, unable to put into words exactly quite what I'd been feeling. I somehow felt differently after all this than I'd felt on the day he went missing. "And I fear that he's dead," I said softly.

She took my arm. "I don't think so."

"Why- what can *you* know?"

"I know one thing." Her face briefly twitched with pain, and letting go of my arm, she hitched her skirts, rubbed her calf. It was blotchy with angry red flea bites.

"Now come along." She let go of her skirts. "I'll take you and show you my secret."

Now flip over and read
Robert's side of the story!

ROBERT'S STORY

The poor girl coughed and sneezed.
I veered back in alarm, wondering if she
was afflicted? I saw her rubbing
her arm and noticed little red
blotches all the way from her wrist
to her elbow. On the ship I had seen
the same thing – but what did
that prove? They were only flea bites...

ROBERT'S STORY

READ RACHEL FIRST
THEN READ ROBERT

KINGFISHER
An imprint of Kingfisher Publications Plc
New Penderel House, 283–288 High Holborn
London WC1V 7HZ
www.kingfisherpub.com

First published by Kingfisher 2006
2 4 6 8 10 9 7 5 3 1

A CIP catalogue record for this book
is available from the British Library.

ISBN-13: 978-0-7534-1326-5
ISBN-10: 0 7534 1326 4

Printed in India
1TR/0206/THOM/SGCH/80GSMSTORA/C

MY SIDE OF THE STORY

ROBERT'S STORY

PHILIP WOODERSON

KINGFISHER

Have you read Rachel's side of the story?
If you haven't, flip back and read it first; if you have,
you can now read Robert's side of the story!

Chapter One

The latch rattled. "Are you in there?"

My mother's voice sounded anxious.

It was only half an hour ago I had heard the clatter of hooves and voices in the still air. So few travellers passed this way, I went hurrying out of the hut, convinced someone must have betrayed me. Though by the time I looked down from the ridge, the lane to the village was empty, with only that faceless corpse creaking about on the gallows.

Only? It haunted my dreams.

So much for my grand ambitions to get away from this place and make my fortune in London! I seemed to have come full circle.

The latch rattled again, and I opened the door. This time Mother wasn't alone. Someone was close behind her. John Hopgood's daughter – Rachel!

So Mother had been right. She had begged me to wait rather than trek down to London. The Hopgoods would turn up, she'd promised, escaping the plague in the City. Now I realized I'd seen them last night, going along the lane. At the time I'd thought they were country folk on their way home from the fields.

Rachel looked tense and anxious. Was her father angry, I wondered, at the way I had disappeared?

Before I could ask, she told me how she'd seen me watching them. "You were up on the ridge?"

I nodded.

"I couldn't believe it was you though, because we all thought you were dead. I thought I'd seen some sort of phantom." And then she dodged round my mother, thrusting out her arms to give me a desperate hug, as if we were long-lost friends. Which I suppose we were in a way, though hardly the closest of friends.

I found myself patting her back, mumbling about how sorry I'd been to leave without any warning.

"Why, where have you been?" she demanded. "They tried to drown you, I know that much. Someone fished you out of the river?"

I shook my head in amazement. I didn't know what she was saying. "I've just been here for two weeks, that's all." I gestured at my mother. "She said you'd come here. And you've made it."

"But Robert, three months have gone by!"

I stalled, not finding it easy to talk about this, not now. "I should tell your father what happened before I tell anyone else."

She screwed up her nose, irritated. And peering over my shoulder, she frowned at my squalid abode. It was only a ramshackle woodsman's hut, where pigs had been kept last winter.

"We have to be careful," my mother explained. "His stepfather hasn't been told, you see, that he's back in the village. "

"No one else must know either," I added.

Rachel carried on looking about – at the heap of straw in the corner that served as a rustic bed, the crude table piled with my papers, the crust of a loaf on a plate. But then she surprised me by grasping my wrist. "They couldn't have followed us here. It's all right. We escaped from our house in the night."

"*They*?" I glanced sideways at Mother, who hastily shook her head as if to reassure me. The girl had no clue to my secret.

"Yes, *them*…" Rachel laughed at the word. "I can't really hate them now, not any more. Seeing as they haven't killed you!"

I tried to laugh too, tried to put her at ease, though actually I was just baffled. "Who do you mean?"

"Pethbridge and Beastor!"

Now I was even more puzzled. "They didn't much like me, I grant you that. I wasn't important enough, but..."

She blinked with surprise. "Be straight, *please*. What did they do to you, Robert?"

I gawped at her in amazement, stunned by how much she'd changed. I'd always been slightly wary of her, though not for being like this. More for giggling behind my back with Jess, the servant girl. That was a shame as I'd liked Jess a lot, before Rachel gave her the notion that I was too vain and pompous to want to waste time with them.

"I've been on the run," I admitted. "But not from those two, more's the pity. I think I'd have handled them, Rachel."

She didn't seem very convinced. She came out with a garbled story about a bolt of fabric Pethbridge had given her mother. "But then he changed his mind, pretended he'd only loaned it."

"What's that got to do with...?"

"He wanted it back for Lord Beastor. So much, he broke into the house in the night."

"You're sure it was him?"

"He stabbed Father!"

"Stabbed him?"

"Made him bleed, yes. And I'm really sure it was him. I found a button that came off his coat."

And to cut a long story short, she now thought Pethbridge and Beastor had been playing her father along, trying to ruin his business and get him into debt. She imagined I'd found out something, which was why I'd gone missing that day. That was why they'd have tried to kill me, to make sure I kept my mouth shut!

She glared at me. "Why are you smiling?"

As if I would hide in this pigsty because I was scared of Lord Beastor! "I'm sorry, but…"

"If you're so clever, tell me what else it could be!"

I braced myself and I told her. "You saw that man on the gallows? He was hanged for stealing a chicken. I've done much worse, so my fate would be worse if the Navy caught up with me here."

"Why? What do you mean?" She stared at me as if she thought I was raving.

"That day I vanished in London," I said, deciding I'd better be blunt, "it wasn't my choice. I was press-ganged, forced to join the Navy. I got sent to sea. I deserted. If I got caught now, I'd be keel-hauled."

She didn't reply for a moment, as if she was thinking this through and getting her bearings again. She nodded. "Why you were press-ganged?"

Well, why did people get press-ganged? To bulk up the numbers to fight onboard ship, as not enough lads volunteered. "One moment Simon Slop was beckoning me into the tavern. The next three men were upon me, and I was dragged down to the river and loaded onto a rowing boat with several other poor fellows. I expect Slop got a few coins from the gang and thought he'd done well for himself."

Rachel fixed me with her eyes; the same grey blue as the cold North Sea, as if she knew more than I did. "I think Pethbridge gave him those coins. What happened *before* you were press-ganged, when you went back to their warehouse?"

It seemed such a long time ago.

I tried to remember that day, what had happened before I'd been grabbed.

I went with Mr Hopgood to deliver the cargo of cloth. We celebrated in Pethbridge's office. Lord Beastor was there as well. He insisted we sample a faddish new drink. It was made out of ground, roasted beans. It was bitter and tasted disgusting even when honey was added. But anyway, Mr Hopgood left his spectacles there. I had to go back to collect them.

It was about two o'clock. I found Lord Beastor still there, on his own.

In fact he was down on his hands and knees, with one of our bolts of cloth unrolled on the bare, stone floor. He was holding some cloth-cutting sheers.

When he heard me he jumped to his feet, kicking the fabric aside. Then he realized I could still see a great hole he'd only just hacked in the fabric. He said he'd made an inspection and found a 'most vile, putrid mark' that rendered the cloth almost worthless. He said I should tell Mr Hopgood to send a replacement at once.

I promised, but had to explain I wouldn't be back at our warehouse until I'd been down to Southwark. I took Mr Hopgood's glasses, but on the way back I got press-ganged.

"There's no connection between those events. Beastor must have been peeved about his message going missing. Did the bolt get replaced by your father?"

She shook her head. "Not that I heard of. But Robert... what if he didn't like you finding him cutting that hole. He wanted to spoil the fabric, to hurt Father's reputation."

"Oh, nonsense. You just don't like him!"

"It doesn't make sense," she insisted. "There's more to it, Robert. I'm certain."

"Best give the boy time," put in Mother, as if she was in on this too. "Robert's been through a lot. There's no hurry. Besides, dears, I ought to be going. The Parson will notice we're missing."

Rachel drew in her breath. "Mrs Duncan, couldn't you leave me here, please?"

"I don't think that would be wise, dear."

Rachel looked to me for support. But Mother

wouldn't be shifted. She had a duty, she said, while her niece was lodged in our house, to chaperone her in the village. Parson Duncan would surely expect it. I couldn't help giving a chuckle, and somehow that melted the ice.

We talked for another half an hour about what had happened in London while I'd been away. How the plague had tightened its terrible grip, taking both Jess and her brother. And Rachel wanted to know about my time in the Navy. "Another day," I said firmly.

"Why, don't be modest, what happened? Were you a big hero, Robert?"

My mother chose this moment to point out the hornet's nest.

It looked like a dusty brown ball. It was seething with big, buzzing insects, all yellow and black. Rachel leapt to her feet. And that was the cue for Mother to say they really must leave now, to try to get back to the house before my stepfather got in a state and sent out a search party for them.

"I'll be back in the morning. I'll bring you more food."

"And I'm coming too," added Rachel.

Chapter Two

I didn't mind time on my own. I'd got used to it, sitting here brooding. Now I went through what Rachel had told me about her father and Pethbridge. If Mr Hopgood had got in a mess trying to deal with Pethbridge, I just hoped he didn't blame me. I had encouraged him, after all, to start selling cloth to his rival. We'd talked about buying French fabrics to widen our range of stock. But so much had happened since then. And besides, he couldn't blame me for all the muddle and upset over their bolt of Versailles. What had all that been about?

With so many dying of plague and the country at war with the Dutch, it just seemed incredibly trivial. I couldn't believe that Pethbridge had broken into their house, let alone stabbed Mr Hopgood. And what was all that about Beastor wanting the bolt of Versailles to give to his uncle, Lord Styx?

The same Earl of Styx with his grand London house and vast estates in Suffolk?

Rachel was only imagining things, overwrought by all she'd been through.

Next morning I woke up early. I gnawed at my dry hunk of bread, watching the sun filter through the green leaves, rehearsing in my mind how I could reach Mr Hopgood without encountering my stepfather.

I couldn't live here much longer. Very soon the weather would turn, and October would bring chill frosts. I wanted to go back to London. I was willing to risk the plague. But that would depend on him being prepared to take me back as his clerk. And that would depend on Rachel preparing the ground for me slightly, so he would come out and see me.

Where was Rachel? I waited all morning. Neither Rachel nor Mother turned up.

The sun was behind the trees in the west before I heard footsteps approaching. I was in a bad mood, I was hungry. But Rachel's hands were empty.

"I've just managed to slip away, by myself."

"Where's Mother? I thought she told you she needed to chaperone you!"

"Listen, Robert." She gave me the strangest of looks, and I thought she was going to start about Beastor and Pethbridge again. But no, she spared me this. She came and sat close beside me. "I'm worried about your mother."

"With my stepfather?"

"Not exactly. I mean, yes, they had a quarrel last night. He wanted to know where we'd been, and she wasn't going to tell him. But this morning she didn't seem well. I thought she was just upset, you see, but…" Her voice had a strange little quiver. "I missed what I ought to have noticed. My own mother makes so much fuss all the time, like this morning she claimed to be sick. But your mother might be really ill. She took to her bed an hour ago. She was asking after you, Robert. I think you should come to the house."

The village was less than a mile away. I didn't want word to spread that I was back from my travels, but now I broke into a run, with Rachel tagging behind me, not caring if everyone saw me.

I burst into an empty kitchen and went thumping through the house, with only one thought in my head: how I would find my sick mother.

But first I found Rachel's mother in front of me on the landing. There was no way to avoid her.

Her jaw dropped. "Lord bless us, the smell. Where do you think you've come from?"

Her rudeness gave me the confidence not to try to explain.

I dodged round her, hurrying on towards my mother's room. :Inside I found Sally, the maid. She gasped with delight. "My dear Robert, a miracle you

15

should be here, just when, oh Lord, you must see for yourself."

She drew me into the room. The hangings were drawn, so the only light came from a couple of candles burning on a side table. It took my eyes time to adjust. The bed was a sturdy four-poster, with curtains closing off the view from here at the foot of the bed. I had to go round the side to try to gain Mother's attention.

In the shadows stood Physic Flatstock. I had known him most of my life as my stepfather's staunch church assistant and the village's man of medicine. He had served in Cromwell's army, first as a humble pike man and then as a self-taught surgeon, hacking off arms and legs at the battle of Marston Moor. But after the Civil War, he'd come back home to his farm. His three sons now did the farming, leaving him free for his 'patients'.

He was mashing up seeds and leaves, using a pestle and mortar. I asked what he thought he was trying to cure, but the old man ignored my question.

It was Sally who filled in the details in her own rustic way, saying how my poor mother had been through the 'hurdy-gurdies'. "She's been hot and cold, pouring sweat and vomiting like a dog, Rob. Now she be as weak as a baby."

My mother was hunched on her side, her hands trembling under her chin. Her face was white on the pillow.

"I was summoned too late in the day," Flatstock said. "All her strength is drained out of her now."

"Can we do nothing more to help her?"

"Would I not, if I thought we should? I know about medicine, young man."

He knew about hacking limbs off, he knew about herbal cures for palsies and menstrual cycles, but if, God forbid, this was plague… "Would a bleeding not lower her fever?" I said. "That's what the surgeon did on our ship whenever a man got too heated. I tell you, I've been in the Navy."

"And I tell you, I have served with the troops, and I have seen more blood than you have. And from my experience, all I can say is the more blood a patient is losing, the less chance he has of surviving."

"I'm sure you knows best," murmured Sally.

"Right now she needs all the rest she can get, so she must drink down this draught. Works every time, it's a knockout."

I was too worried to argue. But once the draught was administered, I got Flatstock out of her hearing, halfway out of the doorway, and asked if he thought

17

this was plague.

"That might be. But giving things fancy names ain't likely to make any difference."

"But is it contagious?" I garbled. "There are others here breathing the air, sir. How is it spread? We must know what it is, what causes it? Doesn't that matter?"

He shook his head, flustered, impatient. "I am not here as God, Master Robert. Though men more learned than I have said such feverish diseases are sent to this world by comets, or else that this 'plague' comes from vapours caused by some great cosmic fart. But I am a simple man, sir."

I grudgingly thanked him and bid him goodnight.

Then I was back in the bedroom, kneeling down by the bed with Rachel close beside me, asking what else could be done.

My mother was hot and damp to the touch. And worse, her skin was speckled with livid little pimples. She was panting yet gaining no air. I told Rachel to draw back the curtain and open the window slightly. We washed her and changed the linen.

She passed into a fitful sleep.

We waited a while, watching over her, with Sally close behind. Sally whispered that Mother had been bright enough, concerned about Mistress Hopgood, at least until after dinner, when she had suffered some upset. The decline had been sudden and dreadful. "That's why we called in Physic Flatstock."

"What *upset?*"

"A tussle with Master…"

"A quarrel, you mean? What about?"

"I wasn't that sure at the time, Master Rob, but now you've turned up, it makes sense. I think they were arguing about you."

"She can't have told him about me." I swung round on Rachel. "*You* didn't?"

"Of course not!"

Sally was shaking her head. And then it came out bit by bit, that after the Sunday service, Master had noticed my mother slinking off somewhere with Rachel; and then this morning, he'd caught her packing up food in the kitchen. "He challenged her, what she was up to. She said there was someone to visit, a poor soul in need of her charity. But Master, he stayed suspicious. Kept plying her with more questions. The poor lady couldn't answer. Then Master got angry, accused her of being a woman possessed."

I felt a great well of anger. "I'll tell you what has possessed her these years — it's him, the arrogant tyrant!"

A voice boomed from behind us. "The devil!"

We swung round. The door fell open, revealing my stepfather jutting his jaw. His eyes had that seething fury I recalled from his Sunday sermons (as well as my regular beatings). The sort of boiling anger he could build up over two hours, fixing that steely gaze on anyone in the congregation not giving him total attention.

"What are you doing back here in my house?"

His tone was as sharp as a spear. I stood up and faced him. "My mother-"

"I know about her, boy. Come hither!"

He beckoned me out of the bedroom and down the stairs to the hallway, where Mrs Hopgood stood watching, caught between horror and gloating.

The study was just as it had been six months before, when I'd announced I was leaving to seek my fortune in London.

The same upright chairs; the scrubbed table, bare except for his Bible, a hefty leatherbound volume, always open so he could read it whenever he might have felt tempted towards 'idle, godless thoughts'. The walls were plain white and the stone floor was bare, so when he knelt to pray he could suffer the cold on his knees. "How long have you been hiding from me?"

I wondered how much he knew, how much he'd prized out from my mother.

"The woman has kept your secret, and fed you, though she has denied it. When you left here for London, I told you don't ever come back. I disowned you!"

I felt my face flush. I tried to breathe deep. "Don't worry, I only came back to see her. I wouldn't have stayed this long, sir, but I needed to wait a few days so I could meet my employer."

"You let him down too. You ran off."

"I was press-ganged, sir, into the Navy."

"So why are you not still at sea?"

I dipped my head. "I... deserted."

He smiled at this revelation. "A *third* time you ran away then. As you will keep on doing, boy, until you face up to your conscience. Your wilful ways take you further from God. Submit yourself to His service."

"I will leave in the morning, won't trouble you more."

"Leave your mother to pay the price?"

I glared back at him. "No, I will take her, as soon as she's able to walk. I'll care for her somehow, if you won't."

"Idle words from a lying toad. The woman is sick for her sins."

"She has done nothing wrong, sir. Blame me."

"I have no concern for your soul any more." He stepped back. "Get out of my house."

I pushed past, out of the study. I just needed air, open space. But instead I met Mr Hopgood coming out of the kitchen.

His eyes nearly popped. "My dear Robert." He grasped hold of my hand. "What a blessing!" He gave me a sheepish smile. "We all feared the worst. I'm so glad you're alive. I'm only sorry your mother…"

"I'm sorry as well, sir. And sorry as well I left your house like I did. It wasn't my choice, I assure you of that."

He nodded. "Rachel has told me. But no need to talk about that at this point. You'll be welcome back. You must know that."

I thanked him and broached my idea of returning to London forthwith, or as soon as my mother was better, so I could do my duty by him and seek to protect his possessions. And then Mr Hopgood surprised me. "I'd count it a blessing, Robert, if you would stay up here with us. I so like our conversations, and as for my daughter, you wouldn't believe, she's been quite a different person since she's seen you again." He twitched a grin, squeezing my wrist extra tight. "I'd come to depend on you, Rob, like a good, honest son. We've all missed you."

I gulped an answer. "I'm humbled… though I don't think I'm able to stay because…"

I saw a shadow cross his mild, kind face, but I carried on. "My stepfather..."

Then I heard Mrs Hopgood exclaim from behind, "Glory, John, what is the meaning? You heard what our host, Parson Duncan, said about this young man. You can't think of taking him back now?"

"Why not?"

"When we've got a young daughter like Rachel?"

Mr Hopgood wiggled his eyebrows. "Dear, don't be a ludicrous ass."

In all the time I'd lived in their house, he'd never made such a remark. I swung round to catch her reaction. For once Betsy Hopgood was speechless. Her mouth was wide open, lips wobbling.

And somehow this gave me confidence to go straight back up the stairs.

Chapter Three

Rachel kept me company.

We sat either side of the bed.

She wiped my mother's face with damp towels, and we tried to ease her breathing by helping her sit upright, though with all the gasping and choking for breath her body kept sliding back down. And as the night wore on, she seemed to get smaller and older. It was as if she was shrinking away, drained of all hope of survival. Or else, as I couldn't help thinking, she had no great will to live because her life was so bleak here.

Though in her last gasps she was calling out, asking to see her dear husband. So Rachel dutifully went downstairs, only to come back again, whispering that Parson Duncan could not be disturbed. "He's praying for her soul, not her body," she whispered.

It was a most terrible end. Like drowning upon dry land, for the fluids all came from within, filling her lungs with foamy spume that was streaked with bloody flux.

Afterwards there was a strange sense of peace, as if her soul was set free.

The silence was only broken by an owl hooting

out in the woods. Perhaps the very same owl I had heard every night from my hut. I felt too upset and tired to move. It was Rachel who drew the linen sheet over my mother's face.

"Shall I tell your stepfather, Robert?"

I shook my head. My duty was surely to tell him, hard as that would be. The last thing I wanted to do was give him the satisfaction of thinking I'd failed in my duty. Confounding his expectations mattered to me, even now, with my dear mother's body still warm.

If only my father had lived...

If only she'd not had to marry again...

She had been such a good, kind mother to me, I'd simply taken for granted that she would keep my secret and shelter me here at Saxton. Yet with her passing so suddenly, I'd not even managed to thank her.

I got up, turning round to see a shadowy figure wavering in the doorway. Too tall to be my stepfather, I saw it was Mr Hopgood. Perhaps he'd been there a long time. He murmured a few words of prayer, putting his hand on my shoulder. Rather meanly I found myself thinking, at least his 'ludicrous' wife was bound to keep out of the way. I remembered from back in the spring, how firmly she'd objected when her husband had tried to encourage her to visit an old friend who was dying. She'd declared she would rather remember her friend as she had been in her prime, not spoil her pleasant memories by seeing her so enfeebled.

But that was nothing, of course, compared to my stepfather's absence. I carried on down the stairs.

The door to his study was standing ajar. A single candle was burning.

The Bible was open before him at some chapter in the Old Testament.

He must have heard me clear my throat, but he turned the page and kept reading.

"Sir," I said, "I have very sad news. My mother, your wife…"

He looked up, but only to face his reflection in the black panes of glass in the window a few feet away.

"I don't wish to hear it, not from your lips. For you were the cause of her suffering."

I gulped, unable to form a reply.

"Indeed." He swivelled round, a strange sly smile on his lips. "Having the nerve to come back here, to tempt the poor woman, like Satan. Don't deny it, you led her astray. She lied to me and deceived me, rejecting the chance of telling the truth even when I asked her directly. Because she knew what my verdict would be. Now the good

Lord has judged her guilty, and that's why He's taken her from us. I suggest you go now, and think on it."

I went wandering back to my hut in the woods in a mood of deep misery, stunned by the double blow of losing the only person who had cared for me as a child and being blamed for it by my stepfather.

Sitting alone in the dark, I wondered what he was thinking right now. Or had he gone back to his Bible? At least he had that consolation. I only had my own sorrow.

I tried to suppress my emotions, doing my best to concentrate on simple, rational thoughts, rejecting my stepfather's judgement, doing my best to work out how it could have happened, that my mother had been infected with plague when the rest of the village stayed healthy.

It seemed so unjust, and it didn't make sense. She must have caught it from *somewhere*.

There had been some cases of plague on our ship. Three of the men in our press-gang had come from a plague-ridden street, but I had escaped contagion. Could I have carried it back here? How long could the plague remain dormant? And how was it carried, I wondered – in one's clothing, mixed up in one's sweat? If so, why hadn't she sickened before? I'd been here nearly two weeks.

It seemed unlikely that I was to blame, but this was no consolation because how else had it got here, unless… had it come from London, brought all this way by the Hopgoods?

In that case, why weren't *they* ill? Why hadn't it been Betsy Hopgood coughing her last in that bed?

Chapter Four

I was back at the house, in the kitchen, in time to sit down for breakfast.

My stepfather made no comment, as if even he must allow that a son should mourn his own mother. He sat there spooning up porridge, looking down at his bowl, making no attempt to talk about when I should leave. And afterwards, rather than shutting himself up in his study again, he prowled about in the garden. He accepted respectful condolences from villagers passing by, but he steadfastly made no reference to Mother's real cause of death, dismissing it as a 'vile fever'.

And when we were left alone again, he told us it might be best if none of us spoke of the 'pestilence'. He did not want the villagers put in fear of their lives for one isolated incident. Simply as a precaution, to limit the slightest chance of any contagious matter escaping into the atmosphere, he wanted the funeral held as soon as could decently be. "This afternoon, at two of the clock. I have asked for the hole to be dug."

Mrs Hopgood nudged at her husband.

He cleared his throat. "My wife is concerned… about the… preparations. I mean, for her sister's coffin. I will happily pay for one made of good oak, with suitable fittings and so forth, though surely the village carpenter is going to need time to construct it?"

My stepfather held up his hands. They were soft and smooth as ever. He brought them together in a sharp clap, as if calling us all to prayer. "We don't believe in such fripperies here. We are simple souls, Mr Hopgood. The worms will feast on our flesh in the end, whether we're buried in caskets or sewn up in old linen sheets. What matters far more is where our souls go. Don't you trust in our Lord for salvation?"

"Of course, yes, but even so. I'd have thought..." Mr Hopgood's baggy cheeks flushed, his eyebrows edging up, leaving it to his wife to say in a flat, level tone.

"My poor dear sister... poor Martha..." Abruptly she drew herself up. "My bolt of Versailles, we will use that, instead of your sheet, Parson Duncan. That will save you extravagant costs, and you might be pleased to know it will give me some satisfaction."

I glanced at Rachel. She shook her head.

Mr Hopgood jerked his brows. "My dear, first thing Sunday morning I unrolled it end to end. There wasn't a good square inch, just a great hole near the middle! I threw the thing out, in the yard."

"Why didn't you say so before?"

"You took to your bed. You seemed so unwell.

30

I feared that the news might upset you."

My stepfather made a loud snort. "Good riddance, wherever it's gone to. I've no time for hearing this nonsense!"

But Mr Hopgood blocked his exit. "Before you go, Parson Duncan, sir, I won't be ignored on this subject. I'll pay for the best linen sheet that you have. If need be, off my own bed!"

My mother was buried that afternoon, sewn up in a good linen sheet. Much of the village turned out, well over three hundred people. The funeral was held in the churchyard.

The weather was sticky and damp, though the grass was dry underfoot. My stepfather led the prayers, then made a short dedication. He grabbed the shovel himself and covered her body with earth.

Mrs Hopgood kept dabbing her nose with her husband's white handkerchief. Mr Hopgood looked up at the sky. Rachel seemed strangely distant, much like I felt in fact. As if we'd both seen so much of death – her in London, me out at sea – one more couldn't make any difference. I couldn't relate such a scene to the love I still felt for my mother.

Afterwards, empty and bleak, I walked back to my hut in the woods.

I sat outside with my back to a tree. I didn't feel the rain until I heard a voice nearby, and turned to see Rachel there. Her fair hair was stuck to her forehead. I realized my clothes were sodden.

She said she'd been there half an hour or more, not wanting to interrupt my thoughts, though I had been thinking of nothing.

All at once I felt cold. I was shivering. She guided me into the hut and made a nest of straw, and then she lay down beside me, holding me close, like a sister.

"I'm so sorry," she murmured. "*We* brought it; we must have done, from London. We should never have thought to come here."

I told her it wasn't *her* fault. I knew from my time in the Navy, the pestilence moved in mysterious ways. On our ship everyone had been well for our first week out at sea. Then it struck, as if out of nowhere. So had its victims been carrying it, all that time, unawares, in their clothes or hair perhaps?

She didn't reply for a while. Then she said softly, "Maybe. And maybe if Pethbridge and Beastor hadn't got you press-ganged, you would have stayed in London, and now you'd be dead from the plague. Like my friend Jess. Like poor Toby."

I brushed a strand of damp hair from her cheek. "Fate? Or just random luck?"

She took a deep breath and glanced at me. "You still won't believe me, will you?"

"It's not about if I 'believe'," I said, remembering my stepfather jutting his jaw, so sure he was fit to pass judgement. "I just want to go on the facts if I can, from what I can see for myself. I don't know enough to be sure about much." I took her hand. "Just one thing. I'm lucky no harm's come to you. Or your family," I added quickly. "It was on my mind all the time I was gone, what might have been happening in London. I mean, with the business and so forth."

She sensed my unease. "How do you mean? That's not why you deserted?"

I tried to meet her gaze, but I couldn't answer her question. Her hand brushed my cheek in a comforting way. "So what was it like, spending time on a ship in a battle at sea? You've said nothing."

"I don't want to think about it."

"Perhaps it would help?"

I was shaking my head. But then I did tell her about it.

Chapter Five

I told her about the first week, in a rat-infested dungeon with thirty other poor fellows, all innocent of any known crime but press-ganged like myself.

The food was disgusting – dry bread and thin soup – with nothing else to drink but putrid, stagnant water. A few men bribed the guards to smuggle in food and ale; even paper, ink and quills, so they could write to their loved ones. But the press-gang had stolen my purse.

In fact, life got better when we boarded our ship at Chatham, on the River Medway in Kent. I'd never been on a ship before, let alone gone to sea. It was fine as we sailed down river, but once we were out of the estuary a high wind caught the ship, sending it tossing and rolling, with most of us retching our guts out.

"Our ship had sixty cannons," I said. "There were thirty soldiers onboard, as well as near three hundred sailors. When we weren't up on duty on deck, we had to stay cooped below. We were squashed in with kegs of powder, live chickens, pigs and sheep. The older hands slept in hammocks, but most of us pitched on bare planks. We didn't know how to

34

coil a rope, let alone scale a mast. They just said we'd learn soon enough.

"Our squadron met up with some other ships sailing up the Channel. Together we sailed further east. We went around the Essex coast and out across towards Holland. But then a great storm brewed up. A huge wave took our mizzen-mast off. Twelve fellows were swept away.

"In the morning an order was given to try to limp back to port. A cause for celebration." I grinned. "Next day we weighed anchor at Harwich. But the damage was soon repaired. Then we put back out to sea. We met up with the main fleet off Lowestoft."

"What a sight to behold though," said Rachel.

"Three squadrons. More than a hundred large ships, they were all at full sail," I agreed. "And maybe two dozen fireships."

"What are fireships?"

"Well... they're old hulks. I didn't know what they were for at the time, but we found out soon enough."

Early the following morning, even before the dawn broke, a rumour went round the ship that the Dutch fleet was closing in. Our admiral, the Duke of York, was on the bridge of the Royal Charles. He gave the order for us to engage.

"My task was to help carry shot from down in the depths of the hold to the cannons on the main deck. Each shot was a heavy lead ball. I must have been kept too busy to notice how close we were getting to the action. Then a great thunderous broadside went off. The ship was choked with the smoke. You couldn't see more than two yards. The noise left me deaf in both ears."

"Then what?" said Rachel breathlessly, as if I was telling a story.

I told her it only got worse.

We tacked back and forth, in between the Dutch ships. We kept on firing more broadsides, but now they were firing them back. "You cannot, you *shouldn't* imagine…" Their cannonballs smashed through the walls of our ship. I saw boys no older than me, their faces slashed by splinters, the skin hanging loose in pink ribbons. I saw arms and legs knocked off, still twitching as they hit the deck. I saw the first mate's head smashed through, pulverized like a ripe strawberry. My bare feet were slithering about in puddles of blood, flesh and brains.

"Dutch marksmen, up in their rigging, fired musket-shot down on our gunners, taking them out one by one until there were so many dead that even the press-ganged men were called on to take their places, though none had been trained to fire cannons. We just tried to do what the gunners had done, loading powder and shot, lighting up."

Then bang!, a cannon went off while a boy was still trying to load it. It blasted a hole through his chest. At least his death was instant. Another friend had his belly blown out. I was splattered with God knows what. And while I was trying to wipe this off, he was still squirming about on the deck, trying to push his guts back. He was screaming for twenty minutes or more, though with the noise of the battle no one could actually hear him, and actually nobody cared.

"It was every man for himself in that hell." I broke off, glancing at Rachel. "I went down to the hold for more shot. I couldn't go back. I hid. I just wanted it all to end. Go on, you can call me a coward."

Her finger traced a line diagonally over my forehead from my left brow up to the hairline. "So how did you get this scar?"

"Not from the Dutch." I laughed, but it was a hollow sound. "An officer dragged me out. He hit me with the flat of his sword. He prodded me back up on deck. Not that he lived to report me. He was hit through the eye with grapeshot. And then…"

"Nobody knew what had happened. It was like the end of the world. Masses of stuff raining down from the sky. We were hit by a giant wave. The ship tilted over so far that the cannons were pitched from their mountings. The smoke was so thick it was like darkest night. But then rumours started going the rounds that the Dutch admiral's ship had blown up. One moment it had been there a few hundred feet to starboard, engaged by the Royal Charles; the next there was nothing but boxwood and bodies afloat on the surface."

"What happened?"

We found out afterwards. "It was one of our so-called fireships. It shackled itself alongside. It was packed full of tar and gunpowder. The crew set it alight and jumped ship. It soon got the Dutch ship burning. The fire caught their powder store. There must have been five hundred men on that ship. They fished only five from the water."

Rachel took time to think about this. Though not as much time as I did. "But the battle was won?" she insisted.

"You could say that."

"And after…?"

"It must have been eight in the evening when the Dutch broke off the engagement. They'd lost at least fourteen sunk, and quite a few more set on fire, but the rest of them limped away. They left our ships in a very poor state.

"A gale got up in the night," I went on. "Quite a few of our ships were wrecked. They'd lost their sails in the battle or else their rudders were smashed. They got blown onto the shore. We were lucky – we took in a lot of water, but somehow we made it back. We must have got blown off course though. By the time we sighted land, we were off the Yorkshire coast. We put into the harbour at Whitby. That's where I jumped overboard. It took weeks and weeks to walk back here."

"So what did you live on?"

"I managed. The farmers were gathering the harvest. I worked odd days cutting barley. That saved me from starving," I said. "I still didn't have any money. We never got paid onboard ship. Not for risking our lives," I finished. "But that's no excuse for deserting. '*Running away as usual*,' as my stepfather put it."

"Don't say that." She hugged me more tightly. "Thank God you survived, that's the main thing."

"But what happens now?" I said bleakly.

"You will come back and work with my father, of course, until you find something much better!"

Chapter Six

Alas, it was not to be.

I stayed that night in the hut, hoping Rachel would turn up to see me again in the morning. When she finally came, in the late afternoon, her eyes looked sore, as if she'd not slept.

"What is it now?" I asked her.

She looked at me none too brightly. "Your plans will have to change, Robert."

"Because of your father?"

She nodded.

It took me a moment to understand. Then I had a whole stream of thoughts – that her mother, backed by my stepfather, must have persuaded her father he shouldn't be taking me back because I wasn't worthy, even for that godless calling. But was Mr Hopgood so weak? After practically calling me his own dear adopted son?

Then Rachel... burst into tears.

My time alone made me self-engrossed. It took me by surprise that she could be so concerned. "I'll manage. I'll walk back to London. I might even work for Giles Pethbridge!"

"Is that all you can come up with?"

"I'm saying you don't have to worry. I mean,

you can tell your father-"

She fixed me with a withering gaze. "He died an hour ago, Robert."

This time it was me hugging Rachel. I didn't know what to say. And when I tried to console her, she cut me short. "No, I knew. I knew something was going to happen after last night, walking back."

"Last night, walking back?" I echoed, my voice sounding stupidly shrill.

"I saw that figure again. I saw Death."

"*Death*? Rachel, what do you mean?"

"I saw him before," she murmured. "I saw him in Gracechurch Street. He was tall, all in black, with a hood. I saw him again and again. And then Jess died. So did Toby. And then he was up on the ridge that day, when we arrived here at Saxton."

"That was me, Rachel. Honestly. You've seen no ghost."

"But last night it wasn't you, Robert. I saw him up close. He was older."

I studied her solemn expression. She always had an imagination. Now her eyes were round, her gaze distant, as if she saw something I couldn't.

"So where was this... apparition?"

"He was out on the village green. I called, but he

41

backed away, he disappeared into the shadows. An omen… and now Father's dead."

I tried to calm her, stroking her hair while saying what a good man I thought her father had been. So mild and modest and honest.

She said he had died very quickly, without any gasping or choking, as if he couldn't be bothered to struggle to hold onto life. "He seemed resigned to it somehow… his only concern was my mother."

I dreaded to think how she'd be.

We found her in the kitchen, talking quietly with Sally. She looked drained and pale but she welcomed us both, and when I expressed my condolences she gave a slight toss of her head, as if to make it clear she needed no kindness from me.

I wondered about my stepfather. Sally said he was shut in his study, again. I imagined him, reading his Bible. No doubt he could find consolation in thinking Mr Hopgood had died for his worldly ways. It seemed unfair that it had to be him taking the funeral service. But take it he did, the next morning.

The short service was much like the previous one, except that none of the villagers turned up to mourn a stranger. There was only Sally the maid and us. I'd thought Master Flatstock might be there, to show some respect for his patient, but Rachel said he'd been feeling unwell even while tending her father.

My stepfather made his own feelings quite clear by reading Psalm 49.

They that trust in their wealth, and boast themselves in the multitude of their riches...
Like sheep they are laid in the grave; death shall feed on them; and the upright shall have dominion over them...

Chapter Seven

Afterwards, Rachel and I walked back either side of her silent mother.

Rachel's eyes were red-rimmed from crying, her hair all matted and tangled from being out in the hot, damp breeze. Mrs Hopgood was still strangely calm. She held her head high, lips pursed as if she was deep in thought about what she ought to do next.

My stepfather stayed behind to wait for the diggers to finish, so he could plant the rough wooden cross engraved with the name and a date.

I wondered what he intended. Mrs Hopgood and Rachel were guests in 'our' house. They had no one else they could turn to. They needed some word from him that they would still be welcome. Otherwise, I supposed, we would all have to leave the house and find somewhere else to shelter.

An hour passed before he returned, trudging through the house without a word to anyone. But this time I was resolved not to let him slink into his study and lock himself up with his Bible. I called out to him in the hallway.

He turned, looking cross and impatient, but when I suggested we needed to talk, his cold grey gaze lightened slightly. He beckoned me in. As he shut the door, he muttered, "I suppose you'll be changing your plans now. You'll need some other employer to help make your way in the world. But say what you will. Keep it brief though."

I said there was plenty for which I felt shame, but nothing to do with the Hopgoods. "I never ran away from them, from doing my duty there. I owe Mr Hopgood a debt though. Now he's dead, I must help his family. They have no other protectors."

I felt a bit presumptuous, making that claim for myself. But my stepfather didn't contest it. Instead he rather surprised me by saying he only took issue with me running away from Saxton. "Your mother needed you here. As for you quitting the Navy, I can make no objection to that. You had a right to desert. The Commandment says 'thou shall not kill', and this is an unjust war. The Dutch are fellow Christians, Protestants like ourselves, and the squabble is all about commerce, as such it should not be supported."

He gave me a sharp, darting glance that might have been almost playful. But his next words were even more startling.

"I have a confession to make. The last time you were in here I accused you of being the instrument leading your mother astray. Now Hopgood is dead, for what reason? The man did not serve the Lord with his heart, but would the Lord smite him for that?" His tone was quiet and thoughtful. "I have to admit, I assumed so. But I have learnt something within the last hour that has altered my view on this subject. I say to you straight, we're all sinners. My sin has been one of false pride – claiming to know the Lord's will!"

"What has happened to change your mind then?" I asked.

He squeezed his hands tight together. "I heard before the funeral that Flatstock was sick with the plague. I tried to visit him on my way home. He'd died before I arrived there. His wife is now suffering a fever. Where will it end? Where's the justice?" He jutted his jaw. "No, don't answer. The Lord moves in His own mysterious ways. It is not for us to pass judgement."

I nodded, remembering the men on the ship blasted to bits in that battle. "We should use our minds rationally," I said, "to try to work out the cause, the physical cause of this sickness, to try to control the contagion?"

He eyed me not unkindly. He didn't reply straight away but squeezed his hands tighter together, making the knuckles crack. "It can't be denied, with Flatstock dead, the plague is no friend to good men. I was arrogant to think otherwise. So yes, it's our Christian duty to try to hinder its progress, to stop the pestilence spreading." He gave me a guarded grin. "I shall need to give it some thought too."

"And what of the Hopgoods?"

"They're welcome to stay, until they can go back to London."

I thanked him for this show of kindness.

"So Robert," he grasped my hand, "I'll be calling a meeting tomorrow for all our congregation. You were born in this place, baptized in the faith, so if you are still in the village I'd welcome it if you can come." He patted my back. "Air your views."

I spent that evening alone, back in my hermit's hut. Rachel had said she needed time to be alone with her mother. I had my own thinking to do.

My stepfather's change of heart left me disarmed and confused, but I'd been through this in the past more than once. He could manipulate people.

It wasn't as if his position had changed as much as he claimed. He was still trying to find God's will. He still assumed God was behind the plague, if not using it as a weapon for punishing unbelievers, then for some other purpose. To carry a general message perhaps, for men to mend their ways.

This made no sense to me.

If the plague had a physical cause, it would help to know what it was in order to try to stop it taking any more lives. If we succeeded, I wondered, would God be angry with us if He was a merciful God? Deduction seemed more important right now than theological thinking.

My father had left me copies of the works of the great Francis Bacon. I didn't know whether he'd read them. Mother thought they'd been given to him in payment for a portrait. The feckless nobleman who'd commissioned it had protested he'd run out of money. But anyway, they were my only books, and I'd tried my hardest to read them to try to make sense of the world.

Making sense of the world, according to Francis Bacon, required 'true and perfect induction'.

In this case, trying to find out what was causing the plague without making any assumptions, but looking at all the evidence no matter what that might be.

So what did I have to go on?

From my time onboard our ship, I knew for sure the plague could break out far from land. Though whether it was transmitted by touch, or in the air we breathed, or in the food we ate, I had no idea as yet. But I was in a good place to try my best to find out.

Chapter Eight

I set off back to Saxton the next day, deciding to start my enquiries into the causes of plague by visiting the cottage where its next local victims had lived.

The Flatstocks' farm was across three fields, well away from the village. There were rose bushes round the front porch. The air smelt sweet as I knocked on the door, making it extra hard to believe that the plague was transmitted by air, unless through human breath. The Flatstocks had been less exposed to the breath of everyone else in the village than those living close to the centre. Yet they had been singled out to come next, after my dear mother and Rachel's unfortunate father. Of course, Flatstock must have breathed their bad air while tending them at our house. But so had I – so had Rachel.

Flatstock's daughter opened the door.

I could see by her empty expression, any news on her mother would not be good. She ushered me into the parlour. Both her parents were dressed in their Sunday best, laid out on their oak dining table.

I said how sorry I was, but the poor girl was too upset to make much sense, let alone show any interest either in me or my theories. She coughed and sneezed. I veered back. Then she saw the alarm in

49

my eyes. She nervously rubbed her arm. There were little red blotches over the skin in a line from her wrist to her elbow. On the ship I had seen the same symptoms, but what did that prove? Only flea bites.

I asked who else had been in the house since her father had tended my mother.

Only her brothers, she said, along with her cousin Jethro. He lived with his wife and three children on the far side of the village. She thought they were all in good health...

I left her, wondering whether her brothers and cousin would happily stay in good health, and what this might prove either way. They'd all breathed in the same vapours. They must have all touched one another. Did that mean the plague would spread, jumping straight from this house, sparing the neighbouring cottages but striking across the green? Infecting Jethro first, then his wife, then their three little children?

The meeting was called for midday. It was going to be held in the nave of the church, the only place in the village with enough space for so many. Two hundred people had gathered there. They'd all been summoned in person by stepfather out on his rounds.

Every household must have sent someone, and

several families were there in all their variety – from old crones to newborn babies. Quite a few of them welcomed me back. Some treated me like a great hero for venturing out in the world. Others were more suspicious, as if I posed some sort of danger. I didn't tell them I'd been to sea or fought at the battle of Lowestoft!

The older folk could remember the last time the plague had struck Saxton. This was back in the 1630s. It had taken twenty or so, including the rector's son. The village had all been Anglican then, before Parson Duncan had won them around with his sermons on faith or damnation. Were they hoping he'd say enough good earnest prayers to grant them the Lord's protection? Most of them had a wry humour about what the future might bring. They were country folk after all. They toiled by the sweat of their brows, but had to accept that the weather would provide a good crop... or a famine.

As for my stepfather, what would he say? He had no cure for the plague. Would he still try to pass on the blame, to Rachel's father, my mother or me? Or show his new, kinder face?

Rachel and her mother were there. I went to sit beside them. We had little time to talk though, before my stepfather arrived. He was in his black clerical suit, his hands clasped in front of his chest and that satisfied smile on his lips, as if the Lord had kept him informed of all His plans for the village. Such presence brought instant silence. He asked everybody to stand, that he might say a short prayer. The prayer was for guidance and wisdom, to do as Our Lord would wish, that we might live to serve him, but also our brothers and sisters in our village and neighbouring parishes.

This should have made me realize where his thinking was heading.

To start with he wanted us all to know how he had sat up all night, waiting upon the Lord, intent on doing His bidding. He said he had prayed for the souls of his own dear wife, Martha Duncan; and for John Hopgood and Denzil Flatstock. Now he offered a prayer for Hannah, Denzil Flatstock's wife, and also his heartfelt sympathy for the Flatstocks' daughter and sons, who were all here with us today.

"Thus we are reminded anew, we live in the shadow of death."

There was a stern, deadly silence.

"My friends," he was squeezing his palms, his knuckles prodding his chin, "you will know me as a man who does not mince his words, so I must tell you straight. We had hoped plague would pass us by. We have thought of this place as our haven, made into a godly fortress by our trust in the Lord. I must tell you, our faith was misguided, corrupted no doubt by false pride. There was also a lack of compassion. We turned men away from our gates. Ordinary, humble travellers out on the open highway. Yet four people entered our village, each of whom came to my house. This means I have been the instrument in breeching our own defences."

His head was unbowed. He stared round the nave.

"There have been deaths. More might follow. Our task is to work with the Lord to handle whatever befalls us. Does anyone have any comment?"

No one spoke, so I put up my hand. I said our first obligation was to do whatever we could to stop the plague from spreading. Then I had a most basic idea. "Surely meeting like this, all together in this closed place, isn't wise? At least we should talk in the open, outside?"

My stepfather twisted his lips. "It is a fine day. Let's go out then."

There were grunts and mumbled protests, but everyone shuffled outside. Then we carried on the discussion around the two open holes in the ground waiting to take the Flatstocks.

This had the useful effect of making us all more wary. None of us wanted to die. And Jethro Flatstock piped up, "Excuse me, Parson Duncan, sir, but do you mean, now that we've got the plague here in the village of Saxton, we might as well let others come here? I think that's a good idea, sir. If they get fair share of catching it too, it should spare a few local folk!"

This brought a few cautious chuckles.

Then somebody else piped up, "If you ask me, we'd be more sensible to clear out while we still can. Not stay here and see who might get it! I'm taking my wife and the children to stay with my uncle, I reckon. There's no plague been reported out at Nether Hopping."

"That's right," I said, and I told them how things had been in London. "The plague made speedy progress there because of so many people all cooped up together. If everyone here spreads out and tries not to have too much contact, that ought to improve all our chances."

But Stepfather raised his hands. "We must think as Christians, my friends, not as animals fleeing a heath fire. We sinned by manning barricades to keep our neighbours out. But the plague still crept in like a thief, and now we must live with it here. It might have been brought in from London. Or else from our ships out at sea. But we have to bear in mind that our neighbours round abouts have not been infected as we have. So what is our Christian duty? To try to save our own skins, or care about others, my friends?"

There were uneasy nods and grumbles.

"Please think!" He held up both hands. "We'd be taking the plague to our neighbours. Should we visit this evil upon them?"

An awkward silence. Some coughing.

"Are you saying we all have to stay?" Jethro asked.

My stepfather smiled at him mildly. "I am saying, we still have our barricades on the boundaries into our village. Perhaps now the time has come to put them to better use, to keep the plague girded in here in order to stop it from spreading."

There was a general shuffling while some of his congregation tried to make sense of his words.

Rachel's mother got there first, even before I did. With a gasp and a flurry of movement, pulling her shawl from her face, she exclaimed, "I won't be a prisoner! I didn't come all this way to end up a lamb to the slaughter. I've lost my sister, my husband too. Now all I've got left is my daughter."

"So, Madam, what are you saying?"

"We're going whatever you think, sir!"

My stepfather took a step closer. "But where will you go, my dear Betsy? Who has fed you and given you shelter? It ought to be common courtesy to act as your host thinks best. Not to think yourself more important than everyone else in his care."

She stared at him in amazement.

"We must all cast a vote," he went on, "to come to a shared decision, for we're a community here. Hands up, if you please, my good people, all those who are backing my motion."

The most godly put up their hands at once. Another third paused and considered, reluctantly raising their hands, while a quarter or so looked down at their boots, shaking their heads rather glumly, as if they didn't like the idea but had nowhere else to go, so probably had to stay here whatever the others decided.

None of them looked my way. As if, having left the village, they couldn't believe I'd come back in any real permanent sense, so I didn't count in this any more than Rachel's mother.

But my stepfather turned on me. "Robert?"

I should have spoken more clearly to get across what I meant, but I was so stunned by him wanting my view that I couldn't order my thoughts. I blurted, "What? Surely whether we stay, that doesn't mean we have to die here?"

"That settles it," said my stepfather, taking my question as a statement. "A majority wish to remain. Like Robert, I trust in His Mercy. So now let us pray, on our knees."

And down they all went on their knees, as if mesmerized by His presence. *Him* not being God in this case, but their Parson beseeching the Lord to look down kindly upon them.

I thought I was on my own until I saw Mrs Hopgood drag Rachel back up on her feet.

"Come on, girl, we don't belong here."

I held back for a moment out of respect, then thought, well, why should I stay here? I'd already earned his wrath by not falling down on my knees. My stepfather couldn't make any more fuss if I followed them out of the churchyard.

I caught up with them in the lane. And the three of us hastened back to the house and sat down at the kitchen table. Sally was still at the meeting, of course, so we had the place to ourselves.

"Now what can we do?" Rachel asked me. Her tone suggested not much, though before I could try to answer, she said it would be impossible for them to stay on here. "Your stepfather shows his contempt for us with every word, every glance."

"Stop rabbiting," said Mrs Hopgood. "Much better get out while we can, before he comes back and makes trouble."

"Where to?" I said, none too sure Mrs Hopgood meant to include me.

"Back to London. At least that's our home."

"But if you're afraid of the pestilence here, it's bound to be worse in London! The journey itself would be dangerous."

But Rachel said, "Anywhere else then. Come on, Robert, you're so clever."

Her face was set, her eyes wild. I knew I had to say something, come up with a better idea, or her mother would make the decision, and they would be gone without me.

Yet something else held me back. A nagging voice in my head, whispering that it would be wrong to run away yet again. I'd run from here once before, and I'd done it again from the Navy. Whatever my justification, I'd wanted to save my own skin. If we carried the plague, there could be no escape. This time I had to stand firm.

"There's a middle way," I said quietly, doubting

Mrs Hopgood would leap at this suggestion. "Both of you stay in my hut. Rest up a few weeks. You'd be safe from plague, much safer than here or in London! That way we can see how things go."

"Just hope that the plague will die down, you mean?"

"It ought to do that in the autumn, as soon as the weather turns cold."

"But what will we live on?"

"I'll fetch food and drink. The worst thing, you'll both find it boring."

Chapter Nine

We had to move quickly and get out of the house before my stepfather returned. I tried to work out what was needed.

Rachel and I rushed upstairs and dragged down the thinner, top mattress from the bed her mother had shared with her since her father had fallen ill. (The mattress off their original bed had been burnt straight after his death). With this and some blankets and linen, we soon had plenty to carry, even without all their baggage. They needed warm clothes for the evenings. Rachel put on her father's jacket.

I feared Mrs Hopgood was not in the state to walk the long mile to the hut. So I hurried across to the stable and looked at the elderly cart-horse the Hopgoods had brought to Saxton. It was too big for Mrs Hopgood to ride, and the cart was too wide for the path. So I borrowed my stepfather's pony.

We loaded it up with the mattress, then Rachel's mother climbed on its back, helped by the mounting-block in the yard and me pushing hard from behind.

"I haven't a clue where we're going," she said, "but Robert knows best. Always has done."

"She's teasing," said Rachel quietly.

★ ★ ★

It took a quarter hour or so to reach my hut in the woods. The air was soft and hazy, buzzing with flies, wasps and hornets. Rachel's mother looked up at that nest and asked me if I could move it somehow, before she went in through the doorway.

I laughed. "Don't stir up a hornets' nest – that's basic country wisdom. You trouble them, they'll trouble you."

We worked hard and fast, spreading out fresh straw before laying out the mattress. I said I would bring them some books.

"Not boring old Francis Bacon?" said Rachel, "Don't you ever read anything else?"

"He might take some getting into, but it's worth it, the things that you learn, if–"

"Excuse me," said Mrs Hopgood, "but where's Robert going to be sleeping?"

A hornet buzzed in through the doorway, did a circuit and flew out again.

"Why, I must go back," I said gently. "I'll come every day, with provisions."

Rachel gave me a look. "I thought you were going to stay too. You can't share a house with that… monster. He'll force you to say where we're hiding."

"He won't. I'll volunteer it."

"You're mad. We walked out on his meeting!"

"Doesn't matter, you've done the right thing."

She gave me a pitying smile. "That won't stop him making you suffer."

I found my stepfather soon enough. He was back in his study again.

I saw Mrs Hopgood's shawl bunched on top of his Bible, and a note on a small piece of paper, from Rachel, thanking their host. He seemed surprised to see me.

"You forgot something, did you?" he murmured.

Our eyes met. He winced, looked away. "You must have more courage than it first appeared. Or didn't you think I'd be back yet?"

"I am staying here, sir," I told him.

"What for, to undermine me? You helped those two women get out of my reach so they can infect other people, yet now you expect my blessing?"

"I don't come back for your blessing," I said. "If either of them is 'infected', it's best they're not in the village but somewhere in isolation. They're camped in a hut in the woods. But my duty lies here; I'm not running away. I want to help in the village."

He half shook his head, as if clearing his thoughts. "Those women won't fend for themselves."

"No, I'll be responsible for them. I'll take food and

water and leave it nearby. And that's how we'll have to live from now on, all trying to keep our distance to stop the pestilence spreading. I've got some ideas, but I need your help. It's not about preaching at people. We've got to take practical measures."

This seemed to hit home. He eyed me, as if trying to make up his mind if I was a worthy opponent, or merely worth turning his back on. "Without the Lord in your heart, you think you will reap a good harvest?"

I needed to take a few breaths before I could answer him calmly. I told him I'd seen more plague onboard ship than he'd ever seen in his life. "I've got some ideas how to fight it."

"Bold words. But it's easy to talk. You might be trying to deceive me, so I'll let you ride off on my pony with food that belongs to this household."

"I swear to you, on the memory of my dear departed mother. I won't let you down, sir," I promised, trying to keep my voice level.

He pondered a moment and nodded, as if pleased he had got me ensnared. But in the end he agreed, as an act of 'Christian charity', I could go back with some cheese and bread, and even a small pail of milk, as soon as the milking was done.

While waiting, I hurried upstairs and pulled out my volumes of Bacon from their hiding place in the attic. *A Natural History of Winds* could be too complicated, but Rachel might be tempted by some of his literary work, so I took out *The New Atlantis*. No point in choosing a second book. I doubted her mother would read it. In fact, *could* she read, I wondered. Rachel had only managed to learn thanks to her father's enlightened views that girls could learn just like boys. Mrs Hopgood had reckoned this 'hare-brained'.

When I went back down with my satchel, I found my stepfather waiting. He said he was curious to know what I might have in mind, 'talking about taking measures to try to counter the plague'. But before I could answer, he told me what Mr Hopgood had told him, about a general cull on cats that had taken place in London, for fear that they harboured the plague. "Shall we try it in Saxton?" he asked me, a fiendish look in his gaze.

"The only problem," I said, "it might encourage the rats."

"A price worth paying, perhaps? If it denies the devil his tools for spreading this noxious disease."

I saw how his mind was working still. "The captain on our ship had two cats to keep the rats from his quarters. Our mess deck was seething with rats though. I got woken up more than once by them trying to nibble my toes. Mind you, the bites we got from the fleas on those rats gave us more misery."

My stepfather scratched his head. "I think we'd best kill the rats though, just to be on the safe side?"

"Not easy."

"And kill all the dogs?"

"Another thing," I said gently, hoping to change the subject. "In London, they lit fires with damp rags and herbs and spices, intended to drive off the vapours."

"We don't keep spices in Saxton, but use that bolt of not-so-fine fabric for rags, Robert. Anything else?"

"Well, maybe," I said. "The most sensible thing might be to keep infected patients out of range of healthy people. That means, keep the sick in their houses, and those that look after them. We could leave them food outside their doors."

He twisted his lips. "We could try that. Though how can we know for sure who is healthy and who is afflicted?"

I had no answer to this, except to suggest we should take every care, not getting too close to anyone else or touching their possessions.

"This applies to you too?"

"Yes, of course."

"In that case, boy, you must keep to your word, leave food for the Hopgoods some way from their hut, and no more communications."

"Except by letter," I countered.

Chapter Ten

My stepfather let me get on with lighting fires round the village. In return I went along with attending the daily meetings for prayers held in the village churchyard. It was worth it, for after the praying, people expressed their own views about what measures to take and shared their sympathies for those who had been 'afflicted'.

And there were more of these.

Maggie Flatstock had gone down with plague soon after I'd been to see her. The swellings came up at the tops of her legs (or so I was told by Sally). But she suffered no puking and not too much sweat, and after three days she was better. Not so her middle brother. He was dead before he could take to his bed, and his wife and younger daughter died in the following days. His son was afflicted with buboes so big they drove the poor boy mad. He ran naked about the village and threw himself down a well. Only their youngest was spared. My stepfather thanked the Lord for showing His infinite mercy, though it will be Maggie Flatstock who has to look after the child!

Next day I set to work lighting fires round the place, making a pall of smoke that hung over the village green. The barriers were manned night and day to stop people entering or leaving, though my stepfather claimed none would try to because they had sworn an oath upon the Holy Bible. "Whereas you," he said, with a prim little sniff, "only swore on your dear mother's memory."

However, all in all, we were not getting on too badly. Together we set up a system to keep the village supplied with everything we needed. We traded whatever we had in return, such as cloth from the village weavers, farmhouse cheeses and bags of flour. Orders were pinned on a wooden board set up on the village green. Our own goods were put out for collection. Any coins were dowsed in vinegar left in a bowl by the cross.

But before we could mount any cull of the cats, they seemed to sense our purpose and went slinking into the woods, though we caught lots of rats in our traps.

There wasn't much else we could do. Now Physic Flatstock was dead, the village did not have a 'doctor'. Sally said her old aunt, widow Crickley, liked to gather strange herbs in the woods. Her remedies went the rounds. There were other more colourful 'cures', like trying to chill the fevers by bathing in cold cows' pee. The death toll went up day by day.

My stepfather took to tending the sick, mopping brows and holding hands, though mainly to test his theory that once a man had gone down with the plague, whether one lived or died was to do with the state of his soul.

Then the grave-digger died of the plague. His assistant was dead already.

"So now, here's your chance," my stepfather declared, "to be *really* useful at last."

"You want me to work as a labourer?"

He had a bright look in his eyes. "It's got beyond digging graves now. The time has come, I fear, when we must bear in mind that all of us here might die."

I stared at him, not understanding.

"A pit," he said, "deep and wide enough to take everyone in the village. I want you to be in charge of the work. Bearing in mind that the last still alive will have to fill in the hole. Young or old, male or female. You think you can do that?"

I... nodded.

As for Rachel, I kept in contact with her by writing daily letters. I left them in a wooden chest placed beside the stone cross, along with their food and drink. She answered my letters each day. She told me how Mrs Hopgood kept sneezing and wiping her nose, or spending long hours on the mattress.

"*My mother is in such a state of ill health, she hasn't got time for the plague.*"

It sounded as if their worst enemies were boredom and impatience, mainly with one another.

Until the fourth day, when she wrote to say that she had seen him again. She meant the apparition, the figure of Death – in broad daylight. The first time she ran away. The second time she called out to him, and the figure slunk back in the shade.

"*I fear it's another portent.*"

This worried me. Not because I believed this phantom really existed, but because she thought it did. I feared for her state of mind.

I wrote back, trying to distract her thoughts by suggesting she do some more reading. But she wrote the next day that she'd seen '*him*' again, and now she was terrified in case it portended *my* death. I only just managed to stop myself heading straight for the hut.

Chapter Eleven

Next morning, work started before dawn broke.

I had two helpers. We dug for three hours. And even before the sun was up, my face was covered in sweat. The sweat soon got caked with dust from the ground, forming a crusty grey mask. My mind was dulled by the heat, my throat raw dry from thirst. I started to think about Rachel, about my poor mother's death, and then I was fantasizing about how this might all end. It was no cheerful prospect.

I imagined us, still with our shovels and picks, as skeletons in black robes with skulls grinning out from our hoods – all three of us phantoms of death, digging into a pit full of bodies.

When I finally called a break, my helpers were breathless and gasping. I squinted across at the shadows dancing under the trees, and saw him myself there amongst them – I saw Rachel's apparition.

It was then I sat down in the pit. I felt dizzy and weak. Was I going mad too?

Jethro was patting my shoulder. "You needs a good rest, Master Robert. You leave this to us; we can do it."

I forced myself to continue until we knocked off at midday, then I wandered back to the house, feeling light on my feet and far away in my head.

Sally told me a man had been here an hour back. He had come to the kitchen door asking after the Hopgoods.

"Shocked me bad," she insisted. "Didn't expect any stranger, not at a time like this, with the village closed off. 'Mercy me,' I said, 'have you no fear for your life, sir?' You know how he answered? He told me he'd been to the land of the Turks, and come near to death from the plague there, except the Lord God must have spared him. 'No one gets to suffer it twice,' he said. Don't know if that's true, Master Robert."

"What did he look like?"

"Tallish and thin. He had a pale face, pointy beard."

"Wearing all black?"

She nodded.

"And what did you say about Rachel?"

"That she and her parents be gone, I said. And truth to tell, Lord knows where. I never said Mr Hopgood was dead, though naturally, if I had done-" Sally was crossing herself, and with a loud sigh she went on, "I'd have said I have every confidence it will be heaven he's gone to."

I thanked her for this information, then went back out of the house.

So much for the apparition. He was an ordinary mortal like us. But why was he 'haunting' the village?

Who was he and what did he want? I remembered Rachel talking about the first time she had seen him, hanging about in Gracechurch Street outside Giles Pethbridge's warehouse. Now what could he want with us here?

I hurried back through the village, across the green to the cross, hoping to catch this spy in our midst and challenge him once and for all. But there was no sign of the man.

He couldn't be far away though. He'd been hanging round for two days. I thought the best place to spot him again would be out here on the green, where people came and went, trading food with the neighbouring villages.

I made my way to the old stone cross, not sorry to have an excuse for staying away from the pit.

I lay down in the long, dry grass only to find myself closing my eyes. And soon I was dozing away, slipping back into the long lost world of being a child here in Saxton without any troubles or fears when... a shadow passed in front of the sun, and the air felt cool on my face.

A cloud, I thought.

The cloud coughed.

He held out his hand. I could not see his face in

the shade of a heavy black hood.

"My name's Henry Gulp. I'm so sorry, I seem to have woken you up."

I sat up in alarm, ignoring his hand. "You've been watching me, spying on us, following Rachel from London. What is it you want?"

He frowned at this, only to make up his mind with a jerk of his birdlike head. His hood slipped back from his forehead, casting light on his beady eyes. "I will be blunt, Master Robert. I know your name and where you have been, and I know you have worked for John Hopgood, merchant of Leadenhall. He has been smuggling letters to France. I hope you'll be willing to help me."

I stared at the man in amazement. "Why on earth would he smuggle-"

"Very good question. One you might help me to answer."

I was baffled but also intrigued.

"Suffice it to say I have evidence Mr Hopgood has got tangled up in something much larger than he is. Something that makes him a traitor."

I told him he'd got the wrong man. I told him that Mr Hopgood was just a simple cloth merchant who might have got in a muddle exporting some cloth to Boulogne.

"With whom was he trading this broadcloth?"

I shrugged. "A man called Pethbridge-"

"Exactly. And this Giles Pethbridge is backed by a certain Lord Beastor, who found him his contacts in France. You know Lord Beastor's a Catholic?"

"Mr Gulp," I said. "Mr Hopgood never got on with Lord Beastor, whatever the man's religion. So why should this matter to me?"

Gulp pulled a long face. "Master Robert, this village is Puritan, surely? Your stepfather's Parson here?"

"We're not at war with the Catholics," I said. "The Dutch are Protestants, aren't they? And as for Mr Hopgood, he worshipped at St Clements, an ordinary Anglican church. Not that I give a fig either way. I'm a rationalist, Mr Gulp."

He twitched a smile. "As I am myself."

"So what is this all about?"

Gulp gave a big gangly shrug. "Let's talk some more about Beastor. Not much of a Catholic, I grant you that. He is keener on fine lace and brandy. But he needs to keep in with his uncle if he's to inherit his fortune."

"The Earl of Styx?"

"Very good, yes. Now let's go back to the war." He paused, but I said nothing. "Our fleet have won a small battle, you know, but the Dutch will soon strike back. Two factions in the country have dragged us into this mess. A clique of powerful merchants who hope to make great profits if the Dutch lose command of the seas. And those like Lord Beastor's uncle."

"Catholics?"

"You're learning fast. Styx has been the main rallying point for other Catholics at Court. What's more, he's kept in contact with the French court at Versailles. Our King needs money to finance the war. The French might lend him this money, even give military help, but only in return for a secret but solemn promise to make England Catholic again."

I must have been shaking my head.

"You think that unlikely?" said Gulp. "Let me tell you, plenty of people at court shared the King's exile in France. They have a soft spot for the French, as well as the 'old religion'. They would happily persecute Puritans for all being commonwealth men opposed to the King's restoration. Do I make myself clear?"

"No," I said. "This has nothing to do with the Hopgoods!"

"A letter was intercepted at the French port of Boulogne. It was hidden inside a bolt of cloth that came from Hopgood's warehouse."

I shook my head. "What does that prove?" In fact I felt suddenly hopeful. "Pethbridge handled these exports. You should talk to him. Talk to Beastor!"

"We will do, when the time's right. But first we have to catch them out. We want to catch them in the act."

"So why are you wasting your time here?"

"The Earl has been away at Court. He's now on his way back home. He is going to Styx Park, which I'm sure you know is just a short horse ride away. Lord Beastor will be there to greet him. He is meant to bring news from France. But from all we've been able to gather, that letter has somehow gone missing. It was hidden inside some fabric, you see. I heard from the Hopgoods' servants that Mr Hopgood brought a bolt up here for his wife to give to her sister. No doubt Lord Beastor will find that out too. That's why I can feel fairly certain Lord Beastor will be riding over, still wanting to pick up his letter."

I suddenly understood. Without having time to think it all through, I got it. It all became clear. No wonder the bolt of Versailles had mattered so much to Lord Beastor. Poor Pethbridge had been in the middle. "You think Mr Hopgood's their fool?"

"Indeed. He's a fool, but no traitor. And if he co-operates with us, we'll help him to clear his name."

I shook my head.

"Why not?"

"Mr Hopgood can't help you, I fear, Mr Gulp."

For the first time Gulp looked unsettled. "It's in his own interests. He *must* help!"

"My master's not here any more."

"Where is he? Where can we find him?"

"He's dead of the plague, Mr Gulp!"

Gulp saw I was telling the truth. "In that case... I'd better ask you to show me..."

But no, I got there before him. "That's gone as well, Mr Gulp."

He looked suspicious. "What has?"

"You think the length of fabric Mr Hopgood brought up from London concealed a letter inside it?"

He nodded.

"It's too late to find out," I said.

Whatever was left of it now was probably smouldering away on the bonfire a few yards behind us. I pointed towards it. "All gone. But I found no letter inside, Mr Gulp. I had to unroll the whole thing. I tore it all up into rags. And if Mr Hopgood found it, I'd have thought he'd have mentioned it to me."

"He might have done, to his wife. Or else to his daughter. Where are they?"

I kept my eyes on him. "They've gone now."

Gulp took a deep breath, and he puffed out his cheeks. Then suddenly turned away, as if he'd lost interest in me.

I grasped at his arm. "You've not told me yet who sent you here, who is your master?"

He swung back. "It won't concern you, unless…" His eyes gaze went narrow and stern. "If Beastor or anyone else comes here asking after your master, I want you to let me know. I am lodged at the inn at Melford tonight. But if I'm gone, leave me a note. My assistant will make sure I get it."

With Gulp gone, I might have lain down and slept. But there was a funeral in half an hour, and I had to help shift the bodies. And while the funeral was still going on, my stepfather reciting the usual lines, all 'ashes to ashes, dust to dust', I found myself thinking about the strange things Gulp had told me. About Beastor using Pethbridge to smuggle secret letters back and forwards with France. Letters about a plot between the French king and the Catholics at court. How extraordinary – but it made sense though.

I remembered that day last May. Beastor down on his knees, snipping a hole in the fabric. He hadn't been checking for quality. He had been making that hole so he could hide his letter. And I'd gone and caught him at it. Fool that I was, I'd not realized. But he had been scared I might talk. Scared enough to arrange for Slop to lure me into an alley, into the hands of the press-gang.

So Rachel had been right all along. He'd wanted me out of the way.

Much later, back in my room, I sat down to write her a letter. I told her I'd bumped into 'Death', and his name was Henry Gulp. I told her what Beastor was up to, and asked if she'd heard any mention from her father about any letter, and—

"Robert?"

I stopped in mid sentence. I hurried out onto the landing. My stepfather had more bad news to pass on, that the blacksmith and his family were all found dead in Forge cottage.

So seven more victims to bury.

Chapter Twelve

The dawn was breaking yellow and red as I set off with ham, cheese and bread to leave by the stone cross for Rachel, along with the letter I'd written. It wasn't just an account, of course. It was also a gentle warning. For though Beastor's letter might have been lost along with the bolt of Versailles, Beastor had no way of knowing, unless he turned up in the village. Not that I felt too worried. He wouldn't know where to find Rachel.

More likely I'd face him instead, and I had a score to settle.

Autumn was in the air now; the grass was damp with dew. Local wisdom had it the plague would die down as soon as an east wind blew. Or would it go on through the winter, so long as there were still people alive on whom it could continue feeding?

I looked down at our hole in the ground. We had dug out a trench six feet wide, starting close to the hedge on the left and stretching across to the right, a total of twenty five feet. Two thirds of this was already half filled, with just enough soil shovelled back to cover our first sixteen bodies. Then I noticed the one at the end had been disturbed in the night. The soil had been scattered, the sheet torn away, exposing a mangled leg. A stray dog must have got in our pit. I wondered if feasting on plague-ridden flesh would give the dog plague. How to tell?

I hastily covered the damage before setting to work.

It seemed like an age ago that Mrs Hopgood had worried about getting her sister a coffin. We didn't even bother with winding sheets. We just shovelled in some more lime to help the bodies rot quicker.

Now we had to extend the trench to make space for ten new bodies. We could bury the adults two deep and lay the children on top, probably sideways on. This meant extending the trench by another six feet at the least.

My arms and shoulders were bruised and numb as I started hacking away. My younger helper, Matt Tiddle, was looking as tired as I felt. His shovel was propping him up. "It's just us two digging today," he declared, as if he thought I'd not noticed.

"Where's Jethro, still in his bed? Lazy swine."

He gestured down at the ground.

Only then did I gather his meaning. We'd need space for one more body.

"What's funny?" said Matt.

Was I laughing? I felt as if I was dreaming, no longer touched by all this. But I carried on wielding the pick for two hours, while Matt shovelled out the loose earth, and at last it was time for our breakfast. Matt chewed away on a thick crust of bread, but somehow I didn't feel hungry.

Had Rachel opened my letter by now? I wondered what she would think.

We carried on for another three hours. It got worse with the heat and flies and the gathering stench from the trench. But somehow we did it. We paced out the space. We even checked its width by lying down side by side, eyes blind in the hazy hot sun. Then a blowfly buzzed into my open mouth, and I choked on it, swallowed it down. And as I sat up I was gasping for breath, and my vision dissolved into darkness awash with exploding stars and…

"You all right, Master Robert?"

I blinked, trying to focus on Matt's worried face. I mumbled that I was just thirsty.

We got up. He dusted me down. And clambering out of the pit we went our separate ways. Him going back to his cottage to stoke up on more bread and ale. Me heading across the green. I had an intuition that Rachel had answered my letter. I wanted to know her reaction at finding that 'Death' was a spy.

A letter was in the chest. I tore it open and read it

at once.

'*Dear Robert. I am so worried. Why didn't you leave a letter today? Did someone else bring the food? I fear for your health. Please reply when you can. I just could not bear to imagine…*

Sitting down on that same grassy bank, my limbs were suddenly heavy. I tried to carry on reading, but beads of sweat made my eyes sting, making it harder to focus.

'*…imagine you taken unwell. I'm still afraid of the figure in black, though Mother still hasn't seen him. She thinks I am losing my mind. At least this morning we could agree that both of us heard horses. They were going by down on the lane. Except this time it was Mother who seemed to imagine things. She claimed she heard Lord Beastor's voice! As if he would want to come here! I do hope Mother's not sickening…*'

Already?

He'd wasted no time.

And if Lord Beastor was here, he hadn't come as a foolish fop addicted to lace and fine brandy so much as a terrified traitor in fear of having his head chopped off if his part in this plot was uncovered.

Then I had an even worse thought.

Supposing he'd opened this chest? He would have

found my letter. It was addressed to Rachel.

If so, he'd have guessed she was hiding close by. Which meant he was sure to go looking, delighted at being spared from entering our plague-ridden village.

I staggered back on my feet. I needed to warn her, and quickly.

I set off at a run through the wood, only to slow to a walk and finally grind to a halt. I needed to get my breath back. My legs felt so heavy, so clumsy. I stumbled, not on a root or a branch, but one foot over the other. I was down on the ground with dirt in my mouth. I crawled. I grabbed hold of a branch to help me heave back on my feet. I was tottering now like a cripple.

Sheer willpower kept me upright. I got to the hut. I called out.

No answer.

I opened the door.

Chapter Thirteen

The food I had left this morning was still set out on the table, alongside *The New Atlantis*. A blade of grass marked the third page. Their bed was rumpled. The bolster still showed indents left by their heads, with stray fair hairs on the linen. A hornet was buzzing against the glass. But neither of them was here.

I sat down in my old familiar chair, feeling the need to rest. I gazed out of the little window at the familiar view. The clearing was dappled with sunlight. And for the first time it came to mind that the beech leaves were turning yellow. And in that same moment I realized that if I stayed waiting for Rachel, I'd not be back in time to help load the cart with fresh bodies.

Where was she? Her jacket was missing, the one that belonged to her father.

I staggered back up on my feet, intending to write her a note. I had to grab hold of the table. But as I tried to steady myself, the blood rushed into my head, making a roaring sound in my ears.

The next I knew, the light seemed dull.

I was sprawled across the mattress, staring up at the rough, thatched ceiling.

My stepfather would be waiting. He'd be wondering why I was missing. He'd deduce that

I'd 'run away'.

My head was aching, my guts churning round. I felt a sharp twinge further down.

I ran my fingers over my groin and felt hard, swollen lumps. And for the first time it came to mind that I was much more than tired.

And then I heard voices outside.

Was I awake or dreaming? I was flat on my back. I saw their distorted shadows flitting about the ceiling – two ghastly figures with great hooked beaks. They looked like sinister devils.

I tried to sit up, to escape them, but they reached out and clasped my shoulders and knees, forcing me down on the mattress. And as my head hit the bolster, my mouth was forced open wide and an oily rag stuffed inside. It tasted of camphor and nutmeg.

They were talking now. One was Beastor, telling the other to do what he must, "just make the wretch talk, Doctor Bead."

The doctor held one of my drinking pots, its open end cupped in his hand. He was wearing thick black gloves. From within I could hear a fierce buzzing. The pot came down on my belly. Something stung me. Hornets! I tried to scream, only to end up choking.

Again I heard Beastor demanding, "The

Hopgoods, where are they hiding?"

The wooden mask muffled his voice. Only his eyes were real, glinting with evil intent. He pulled out the rag, and I gasped for breath.

"Mr Hopgood is dead of the plague. You've left it too late."

"The boy lies, sting him some more, quick, Doctor!"

The doctor was shaking the pot, popping it hard on my groin.

I yelled, but the noise was muffled by the rag stuffed over my lips.

"No more for the moment," the doctor declared. "Apprehension is worse than the pain. He'll talk in due course, and when he is done," he hissed in my ear, "I can help you. You value your life? Let me cure you. Or else you will die of the plague."

"Or a knife in the guts," Beastor muttered, angrily turning away.

With my eyes screwed shut, I felt helpless. I felt completely alone. Though out of my deep despair, aware I was sick with the plague, probably close to death and close to ending up in the pit I'd dug myself that morning, a bright revelation came to me – that Rachel must have escaped.

Despite all the pain I was smiling, floating up on

the ceiling, leaving those devils behind.

And when I next opened my eyes, the two men were sitting across the room, either side of the table. Beastor had his mask tilted up. He was taking a swig of brandy out of a silver hip flask.

But then the latch rattled. I tensed. Someone was opening the door. I felt a cold breeze on my face.

Who else could it be, except Rachel?

I managed to spit out the rag. I screamed, "No! Run while you can!"

Rachel didn't run. Instead she came forward and *smiled*.

Was I hallucinating? I couldn't see much in the gloom, only the looming shadows given off by the lamp she was holding, its candle flame flickering wildly, leaving her hazy behind it and her shadow on the wall bigger and much more forceful.

Beastor was up on his feet now, drawing his dagger.

But Rachel stayed still, holding her ground. Then she spoke. But this wasn't her; I had got confused. The voice belonged to a man.

"May I ask what you want with my stepson?"

I heard Beastor's proud braying tone, insisting he came here by right as nephew of the Earl of Styx, who owned all the land in these parts. He said he would not be addressed in that way by 'a clod-plodding, Puritan peasant'.

Then the doctor was speaking, more gently, saying there need be no cause for cross words, for he was a medical man and the boy was grievously sick. "It is lucky we happened to be passing by. I can tend to him, my good sir, as the Samaritan did. But His Lordship has one small request first, for something belonging to him. It got tangled up in some cloth by mistake. We believe Mr Hopgood might have it."

"Where is it?" howled Beastor. "I want it."

"In that case," my stepfather answered, not sounding the slightest bit bothered, "you'd better describe it, my Lord."

"The bolt of fine fabric? It's emerald green. The letter's a personal letter."

"From a lady," the doctor said smoothly, "so it could be of no value to anyone in your village. To His Lordship, it's rather important. And delicate too, I should add. Involving a good lady's honour."

Beastor pulled out a big leather purse. "A guinea, if you take me to it!"

And as I faded away, slipping back into unconsciousness, I heard my stepfather say in a light, bright, friendly voice, "I would be very glad of a guinea, as I'm just a 'clod-plodding peasant'. But a 'Puritan' too, as you say. And my conscience would get in the way of taking anyone's money unless I have honestly earned it." He paused and cleared his throat. "I fear your letter is lost, sir. What you ask is beyond my power."

"*Lost*? Who lost it, you clodhead?"

From far away in my feverish state, I thought I heard stepfather... chuckling.

Then Beastor was shouting abuse.

"No, please," my stepfather soothed him, "you were perfectly right, of course. My brother-in-law brought us some fabric. A bolt of very fine fabric. He wanted to please Mrs Duncan. But the Lord in his wisdom, our sacred Lord, must have planted a rodent inside it to save her from any temptation. The dead rat tumbled out, sir, along with some shreds of torn paper. My maid swept them into the hearth. Your lady is safe," he said sweetly. "The rat must have eaten her letter."

And that was the last I heard.

A satisfying silence was wrapping me up like a blanket. And as I drifted away, I had one final sight of my stepfather beaming at Beastor, raising his hands in the air as if to imply that Providence was all around us, here in this hut, and we were mere toys of fortune. Beastor and Bead were gone.

Chapter Fourteen

Stepfather carried me home that night. He and Rachel looked after me well, each taking turns to nurse me, convinced I was going to die.

I was lucky though. I recovered.

It was early in October before I was up on my feet. I was skinny, emaciated, with boils all over my face, but Sally made it her business to feed me back to full health.

From the recesses of my memory, out of that shadowy evening, I tried to make sense of what happened, but only Rachel could help me.

She thought it was all very funny.

She and her mother had made up their minds to hide deeper in the woods after hearing Lord Beastor ride by. They hadn't expected me to turn up. The first they knew about it was later on that evening, when they finally ventured back to find me on their mattress with stepfather mopping my brow.

"So was he telling the truth?" I asked. "Did a rat eat their letter from France?"

"He told the truth as he knew it," she said, as if she was holding back something. "Though whether it came from France I can't say, because all the writing's in code."

I stared at her in some wonder. "You saw it *before* the rat ate it?"

She grinned. "It had a good nibble, but most of it's still in one piece."

"So how did you… When did you…?"

"No, not me. My father must have found it when he went outside and unrolled the bolt. You remember, before your mother's funeral, how he told my mother the fabric had a big hole?"

I nodded.

"That's probably when he found it. He must have shoved it into his pocket, and knowing Father, forgot all about it. But I put on his jacket again when we ran off to hide in the woods. Just as well, it was cold that evening. I put my hands in the pockets and…"

She brought it out to show me. A huge lump of red ceiling wax still encrusted the flap on the envelope where it had been sealed. The letter was lengthy, in bold black ink, but none of it made any sense. I knew what to do with it though.

As soon as I had strength to walk, I set off with Rachel to Melford and left the letter for Henry Gulp.

But now let me write about Saxton. A third of its poor inhabitants went down ill with the plague, of whom more than half were dead before the end of October. By then the weather was cold, and the plague itself died down, though I have to record its last victim was the man who had put such trust in his Lord – my stepfather, Parson Duncan.

We buried him, not in the pit but in his own simple grave with its own wooden cross, in between my mother and his old friend, Denzil Flatstock. I had to speak at his funeral. I paid my respects to a man who had done his best as he saw it. He'd helped stop the plague from spreading to villages round about. And surely he'd helped save my life.

After his death, we stayed in his house until the end of November before risking the muddy roads for a long journey back to London.

By then the plague was spent even there, the bills of mortality showing just a few dozen deaths in that week, and the City was bustling again, nearly as back to normal as possible after such grief and such suffering.

My first task was finding work.

Rachel's mother had made up her mind to sell her late husband's warehouse. She wanted to live in retirement as a respectable widow.

She asked Pethbridge to pay her a call. Rachel was horrified. But her mother was still so impressed by Pethbridge's great success in the trade, as well as his 'patron' Lord Beastor, that she somehow ignored the fact that his 'patron' was gone without trace.

She agreed to sell Pethbridge the business – at a remarkable price, sufficient to purchase a handsome brick house in the pleasant surroundings of Hackney.

Then I had a good piece of luck. I happened to bump into Gulp again while walking past The Sun Tavern. He bought me a tankard of ale, and I asked him about the letter. He said it had been decoded, and as a result the Earl of Styx had fled with his nephew to France. The Catholics were out of favour at Court, at least for the moment. Gulp thanked me. What's more, he offered to find me a post – as a humble trainee clerk, but in the Parliament Office.

That winter was cold. I worked long and hard. But when the weather warmed up in the spring, I took to walking to Hackney most Sunday afternoons to spend some time with the Hopgoods. Rachel hadn't got far with Bacon, not even *The New Atlantis*, but now she was teaching children to read in the local school run by one of their neighbours.

It was good to get out in the country and breathe some fresh air after London. Though little did I know at the time that before the summer was over, I would be lodging in Hackney. For early in September of

1666, London suffered another calamity as terrible as the plague. The City was laid waste by fire. Leadenhall was reduced to ash. Poor Pethbridge lost every farthing.

As for the plague, it had lingered on, but it finally died with the fire. I still wonder how it was carried. I have a theory about rats and fleas, but how could I rationally prove it?